Random Acts

Random Acts

A JOANNA BRADY AND
ALI REYNOLDS NOVELLA

J. A. JANCE

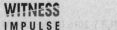

WITNESS
IMPULSE
An Imprint of HarperCollins Publishers

This is a work of fiction. Names, characters, places, and incidents are products of the author's imagination or are used fictitiously and are not to be construed as real. Any resemblance to actual events, locales, organizations, or persons, living or dead, is entirely coincidental.

Excerpt from *Downfall* copyright © 2016 by J. A. Jance.

EPub Edition JULY 2016 ISBN: 9780062499042
Print Edition ISBN: 9780062499059

In memory of my mother, Evie.

"Mom," Jennifer Ann Brady said, "what if you lose?"

Sheriff Joanna Brady and her daughter, Jenny, were seated at a booth in the Triple T Truck Stop where they'd stopped for deep dish apple pie on their way home to Bisbee from a shopping expedition in Tucson. Jenny would be leaving for her first semester at Northern Arizona University in Flagstaff in a matter of days. Because Tucson was a hundred miles one way from Bisbee, both of them had taken the day off work—Jenny from her job at a local veterinarian's office and Joanna from work as well as pre-election campaigning.

Since there had been no panicky phone calls or texts from Tom Hadlock, her chief deputy, or from her campaign manager, either, it seemed likely that things on that end must be fairly well under control.

Somewhere between Wal-Mart—towels, bedding, pillows, sheets, a tiny microwave, and a one-cup coffeemaker—T.J.Maxx—clothing that would have caused Joanna's mother, Eleanor, to have a conniption fit—and Western Wearhouse—boots, shirts, jeans, and a new hat—it had occurred to Joanna that kids needed lots of goods to head off to college these days. That was especially true for Jenny. After being awarded a full-ride athletic scholarship to join NAU's recently reinstated rodeo team, she would also be going off to school with a pickup truck loaded with tack and a horse trailer hauling her relatively new quarter horse, Maggie.

Jenny had insisted that for this shopping trip it should be just the two of them—"like the old days," she had said. The old days in question were the years between the death of Joanna's first husband, Deputy Sheriff Andrew Roy Brady, and the arrival of her second husband, Butch Dixon. During that difficult interval after Andy's murder and before Butch's making his way into Joanna's heart, Jenny had been the only star in her firmament. It had been just the two of them back then . . . well, three really—Jenny, Joanna, and a single dog. Now there was Butch; Jenny's younger half brother, Dennis; and a menagerie of dogs, horses, and cattle, to say nothing of the growing baby bump at her expanding waistline, who was just then pummeling the inside of Joanna's ribs with a series of field-goal worthy kicks.

All in all, it had been a lovely day, but Jenny's question left a somber note lingering in the air over the Formica table in the bustling and noisy truck stop dining room.

"I'm not planning on losing," Joanna said quietly.

This was not a planned pregnancy. Joanna considered herself to be a case study in the statistics that said birth control pills don't always work. And being pregnant at the same time she was running for reelection for the office of county sheriff wasn't that great an idea, either. But she had done it before when she had been pregnant with Dennis, and she was doing it again with Sage. That was what Joanna was currently calling her baby girl, but since Butch wasn't wild about Sage as a girl's first name, that wasn't exactly a done deal.

"Donald Hubble is a cheat," Jenny said, her blue eyes sparking fire. "I'd never vote for him even if you weren't running."

Jenny was eighteen now. This would be the first election in which she'd be able to vote. And the fact that Don Hubble was a cheat—or at least the fact that some of his campaign workers cheated—had been one of Jenny's hot buttons for weeks. She and Butch would go out on a yard-sign trip, only to return an hour or so later to discover that the yard signs they had just installed had already disappeared. Part of the problem with that had to do with the fact that Donald Hubble apparently had more money than God and was prepared to pay his campaign workers, while Joanna had to depend on volunteers, including her fiercely passionate daughter.

"We don't know for sure that he cheats," Joanna said mildly, "although it's clear that some of his workers do."

"It's the same thing," Jenny insisted. "He should know what his people are doing and put a stop to it."

Joanna had been surprised when Hubble had thrown his oversized Stetson into the ring. He was one of those "good ol' boy" types. Cochise County born and bred, he came from pioneer ranching stock, a family that had settled in the Willcox area in the late 1880s. After graduating from high school, he had earned a degree in criminal justice from Arizona State University. He had worked as a police officer in Phoenix for years, eventually rising to the rank of assistant chief before taking his retirement. In the meantime, the deaths of first his grandparents and later his parents had left him with a considerable fortune. He had sold the family ranch for a bundle and subsequently retired to Sierra Vista. Joanna suspected that what had really prompted his entry into the race was a severe case of boredom. Hubble's campaign literature— which Joanna had read cover to cover—said that if he was elected sheriff, he would make the department "more accountable." Whatever the hell that meant!

Bottom line? Joanna had no idea. Law enforcement had become her passion. It wasn't something she'd simply be able to walk away from.

"You still haven't answered my question," Jenny insisted.

Joanna shrugged. "If you make plans for losing, you run the risk of turning that into a self-fulfilling prophecy. Who knows? Maybe I'll decide to stay home with the baby for a while—you know, sit around eating bonbons all day."

"You'd go nuts in a week, tops," Jenny said with a grin. "And so would Dad. The only person who'd be happy about that would be Grandma Lathrop and maybe Marliss Shackleford. Which reminds me, what does that woman have against you anyway? She's always putting snide remarks about you in that column of hers. I wish she'd stop."

Marliss, a reporter for the local paper, the *Bisbee Bee*, also wrote a column called "Bisbee Buzzings" which was the local print and e-version of tabloid journalism. She also happened to be a great pal of Joanna's mother, Eleanor Lathrop Winfield. After Joanna was elected sheriff, it had taken time for her to realize that anything she said to her mother was likely to make it into print through the Eleanor/Marliss connection.

Lately Marliss had devoted several of her columns to the importance of having a "full-time" sheriff as opposed to one with "severely divided interests." The column didn't come right out and say "with a new baby on the way," but everyone in town got the message.

"I wish she'd stop, too," Joanna said. "But it's a free country—which happens to include freedom of speech and freedom of the press, and she's entitled to say whatever she wants. As for what she has against me other than the fact that I exist? That I can't say."

"I suppose Grandma will want to invite her to the barbecue," Jenny said.

Her mother and stepfather, Eleanor and George Winfield, usually stayed in Minnesota until much later in the fall. They were coming home several weeks earlier this time around, traveling a meandering route in their RV, in order to be in Bisbee in time to host a Saturday afternoon going-away kickoff barbecue for their college-bound granddaughter—a party being cohosted by Jenny's other grandparents, Jim Bob and Eva Lou Brady.

On Sunday, Butch, Dennis, and Jenny would caravan from Bisbee to Flag. Butch and Dennis would ride in Joanna's SUV loaded with Jenny's stuff, while Jenny would haul Maggie in a trailer behind her truck.

"Since your grandparents are hosting the party, they

get to invite whomever they want. In other words, don't be surprised if Marliss shows up," Joanna said finally. "And don't say a word of complaint about it, either."

"Right," Jenny said in a tone that implied she wasn't the least bit thrilled.

Lightning flashed outside the windows and a clap of thunder rumbled overhead. While they'd sat in the restaurant, chatting over coffee, a storm they'd earlier seen hovering over the mountains arrived in dead earnest. It was monsoon season in southern Arizona, where late afternoon storms could be fierce, in terms of both rain and dust.

"We'd better go," Joanna said, gathering the check and her purse. "But first I need a pit stop. Getting from here to the ranch without having to find a restroom is about as far as I can make it these days."

By the time they reached the car in the parking lot, the rain was coming down in torrents, and they were both soaked to the skin. They landed in the SUV dripping wet and laughing.

"That was fun," Jenny said, fastening her seat belt.

"Yes, it was," Joanna agreed. "We should do this more often."

With pouring rain blowing sideways across the roadway, the drive took longer than normal. A few months earlier, Butch had surprised Joanna with a new-to-her, just-off-lease Buick Enclave. Her official "geezer car," as he called it. By the time they made it back to High Lonesome Road and found with the dirt roadway awash in water, she was thrilled to be driving a high ground clearance vehicle with four-wheel drive.

Butch had food ready and waiting. After dinner, Jenny was happy to show off her collection of new outfits while Denny contented himself with the new LEGO set Joanna had brought home for him. It wasn't until Joanna and Butch were alone in the bedroom that she was able to show off her own prize purchases. She had bought two new pairs of uniform pants. That day, while she and Jenny had been shopping, a tailor had taken both waistbands apart and installed elastic expansion joints to help accommodate what she knew would soon be a much enlarged belly.

"Believe me," she told Butch. "I got these just in time. Yesterday when I zipped up my uniform, it almost didn't go."

"It sounds like you both had fun today," Butch said, once they were in bed.

"We did," Joanna said, "except for one thing. Jenny's worried about my possibly losing the election."

"We're all worried about the election," Butch replied, "but don't concern yourself. No matter what happens, we'll be fine."

"That's what I told her."

"Have you thought any more about applying to law school?" Butch asked. That was one of the possibilities they had discussed earlier if the election happened to go the wrong way.

"I haven't," Joanna said firmly, rolling over onto her side and then snuggling up next to him. "Because I haven't thought any more about losing. I want to win."

"That's my girl," Butch said. "What a surprise."

He reached around her and let his hand settle on her midsection, where the baby was still kicking up a storm.

"Has she been doing this all day?" he asked.

"All long day," Joanna murmured. "Obviously the kid never sleeps."

But Joanna did. When her phone rang at five past three, it took her two full rings before she was able to grab her crowing cell phone off the bedside table. She sat on the edge of the bed to answer, knowing that a middle-of-the-night call-out like this would probably summon her to a homicide investigation somewhere within the vast 6,400-square-mile boundaries of Cochise County.

"Hello, Tica," Joanna said. "What's up?"

Tica Romero was Joanna's nighttime dispatcher. There was a slight but worrisome pause before Tica replied.

"There's been an incident," the dispatcher said. "Detective Carbajal is on his way to your place right now. He should be there any minute."

An incident? Joanna thought. "He's on his way here?" she said. "Why? What's going on?"

"It's an MVA," Tica replied reluctantly. "He'll tell you the rest when he gets there."

A motor vehicle accident? Joanna thought with sudden dread. Her first thought was that Jenny had pulled a wild-haired teenaged stunt, snuck out of the house for some reason, and had been involved in an accident. But where? And how badly was she hurt?

Without pausing long enough to grab her robe, Joanna sprinted out of the master bedroom and down the hall to Jenny's. She flung the door open and switched on the light, expecting to find Jenny's bed empty. It wasn't.

Jenny was right there with her deaf black Lab, Lucky, on the floor beside her bed.

Jenny sat up, rubbing her eyes. "Hey," she said sleepily, "what's going on?"

Before Joanna could answer, the doorbell rang. That awakened Lady, her rescued Australian shepherd who now slept in Dennis's room, and Lady's frenzied barking automatically awakened Dennis. With the whole household, including Butch, now fully awake, Joanna zipped into the bedroom to grab her robe.

Who can it be? she wondered. *Please, God, not one of my deputies. I can't lose another one of them.*

By the time she reached the living room, everyone else was already there. Butch stood at the end of the hallway with Dennis on his hip. Lucky may have been stone deaf, but since Lady was barking her head off, he immediately followed suit. Jenny, also in her robe, stifled both dogs with an urgent hand signal. Obviously Lady had learned a thing or two while Jenny had been training Desi, the hearing assistance dog Jenny had recently turned over to his new ten-year-old owner.

Joanna finished tying her robe and then flung open the door, where she found Jaime Carbajal standing on the front porch. She shoved open the security screen for him to enter. "Come in," she said urgently. "What's going on?"

"It's your folks," Jaime said simply.

"My parents?" Joanna asked stupidly. "George and my mother?"

Jaime nodded numbly. "Yes," he said.

"Are they dead?"

"George is," Jaime said quietly. "Your mother has been transported to a St. Gregory's Hospital in Phoenix. She's undergoing surgery right now."

As sheriff, Joanna had done her share of next-of-kin notifications. Some people simply collapsed when they heard the bad news. Some people screamed. Some people fell to their knees as if in prayer or waved their arms as if the terrible words were a swarm of Africanized bees. Joanna took two steps backward and then leaned against the arm of a nearby sofa as Jenny gasped behind her. "I can't believe it. Grandpa George is really dead?"

Joanna didn't dare look at her daughter for fear of falling apart. "What happened?" she asked.

"Their RV slammed into a highway overpass south of Camp Verde," Jaime answered. "They were traveling at a high rate of speed. They hit a bridge pier at an angle and then careened off the highway and down a steep embankment."

"Ejected?" Joanna asked.

Jaime shook his head. "No, they were both wearing seat belts. The airbags probably helped with the initial impact, but not as they rolled. They were both cut up by flying pieces of sheet metal. Your mother was transported by helicopter to the trauma center at St. Gregory's. I understand she's in very serious condition."

Joanna took a deep breath and tried to focus. "All right," she said. "I'd better go then. I'll go pack an overnight bag."

"We'd better go," Butch corrected. "I'm coming with you."

"Yes," Jenny said at once, suddenly sounding incredibly grown up. "You both go. I'll take care of Dennis. Carol will help if I need it, and so will Grandma and Grandpa Brady."

Carol Sanderson, a widow raising her two grandsons, lived next door in the ranch house Joanna had once shared with her first husband. Surviving on little more than social security, she was glad to have part-time employment as Joanna and Butch's combination housekeeper/nanny.

Joanna wanted to argue, but she didn't. As her eyes filled with tears, she turned to her daughter. "Are you sure?"

"Yes, I'm sure," Jenny said firmly, taking Dennis out of Butch's arms. "The two of you should get going."

"Can't I go, too?" Denny demanded.

"Not this time, little bro," Jenny crooned. "Not this time. Let's get you tucked back into bed."

Turning her back on the living room, Joanna retreated to the bedroom, where she dressed, brushed her teeth, and combed her hair. By the time it was Butch's turn in the bathroom, he had laid out the two roll-aboard bags they kept on the top shelf of the closet, far beyond Joanna's five-foot-four reach. Butch's was already packed and zipped, and Joanna wasted no time filling her own luggage, moving mechanically, holding her feelings at bay.

When she and Butch returned to the living room, luggage in hand, Jaime still stood in the room, a cell phone pressed to his ear.

"I'll go start the coffee and load the car," Butch said.

Joanna nodded. "Go," she told him. "I need to talk to Jaime for a minute."

Moments later, she heard the sound of coffee being ground in the kitchen. She had given Butch a coffee machine for Father's Day. At the time it had seemed incredibly extravagant, and the aroma of brewing coffee should have been wonderful, but it wasn't. Joanna was over the worst of her morning sickness symptoms, but her pregnancy-caused aversion to coffee was still in effect. By the time Butch was finished packing the car, his traveling mug would be filled and ready to go. Butch would need coffee for their upcoming road trip. She would not.

"Okay," Jaime was saying into his phone. "Got it. I'll be in touch."

Jaime ended the call and then looked at Joanna, examining her face. He may have been surprised to find her dry-eyed. So was she. It was as though the news hadn't yet sunk in yet. It would, though—all too soon.

"Are you all right?" he asked.

"I will be," Joanna said, "but how did the authorities know to call us?"

"One of the officers at the scene saw your name on your mother's cell phone's ICE file," he said. "By then they already knew she was from Bisbee. Somebody saw the name Joanna Brady and must have made the connection to Sheriff Joanna Brady. They called the department, and Tica called me. Is there anyone else you want me to notify?"

"No," Joanna said. "If Butch drives, that'll give me three and a half hours to make calls, starting with Chief Deputy

Hadlock. I'll need to contact my brother in Virginia. I'll also need to figure out how to get hold of George's relatives. I'm sure there are some, but I don't know exactly who or where they are."

"It won't take three and a half hours," Jaime said. "I've already made some calls. Deputy Stock will meet us at the Traffic Circle. He and I will give you a police escort from here to the county line. From there, Pima County officers will escort you as far as the Pinal County line, and officers from Maricopa will deliver you to the hospital itself. By the way, I made the police escort arrangements over the phone. None of that should turn up on Marliss Shackleford's police scanner or in her column, either."

"Thank you for that," Joanna replied.

Butch appeared in the kitchen doorway with two metal-clad thermal coffee mugs in hand. Joanna knew that his would contain coffee. Hers would be ice water spiked with lemon wedges.

"Ready?" he said.

Joanna nodded.

"Okay," Jaime said. "Let's be going. Your police escort is all lined up, Butch, so just fall in behind me."

He let himself out. Joanna closed and locked the front door behind him. When she turned to leave, Jenny was standing in the entrance to the hallway, obviously crying. Joanna went to her and reached up to hug a daughter who was now much taller than her mother.

"I can't believe Grandpa George is gone," Jenny whispered into her mother's hair.

"I can't believe it, either. Thank you for taking charge here, and call us immediately if you need anything."

Butch set the two mugs on the dining room table and came over to where Joanna and Jenny were standing, peeling some bills out of his wallet as he did so and adding an all-encompassing bear hug into the mix.

"I have no idea how long we'll be gone," he told Jenny. "Here's some cash to tide you over in the meantime. Use this for groceries or whatever else comes up."

"We'll be fine, Dad," Jenny assured him, pulling away from his grasp. "Don't worry."

Joanna waited until she was in the Enclave with her seat belt fastened and the door shut behind her before she gave way to the tears she'd been holding in check. Butch reached out as if to comfort her, but she pushed his arm away. "Just drive," she said. "Please."

Butch obliged by backing out of the garage and pulling in behind Jaime, who had already activated the red and blue emergency lights inside the grille on his Tahoe. By the time the two vehicles reached the Traffic Circle in Bisbee and Deputy Jeremy Stock pulled in behind them with his light bar also ablaze, Joanna had reached the end of her tears, at least for now. She blew her nose, wiped her eyes, and took several deep breaths.

"I know this is a terrible thing to say, but I'm thankful George was the one who died," she said as they sped past Lavender Pit and on toward the Divide.

"Why do you say that?"

"Years ago he lost both his first wife and his only child, his daughter, to breast cancer. He was devastated.

Losing my mom, too, would have been too much for him. As for Mom?"

Butch glanced in her direction. "We both know she's tough as nails."

Joanna nodded. "Right," she said. "She's a survivor."

"But what on earth were George and Eleanor doing on I-17?" Butch asked. "They were coming from Minnesota. It seems to me they would have come straight down through New Mexico and then crossed over toward Bisbee from Lordsburg."

"I have no idea," Joanna replied.

"And why the middle of the night?"

"Oh, that. Mom told me once that George preferred driving at night. He said it was safer because usually there was so much less traffic."

"Not this time," Butch said quietly.

Nodding, Joanna glanced at the clock on the dash and pulled out her phone. As she'd told Jaime, her first call was to her chief deputy, but Tom Hadlock was already on the case. "Tica gave me a call," he said. "I'll be at the office first thing in the morning, minding the store. You do what you need to do, Sheriff Brady, and don't worry about the department. We'll keep the wheels on the bus in the meantime."

"Thanks, Tom," she said. "I appreciate it."

"Next up are Bob and Marcie," Joanna said to Butch as the first call ended. "It's almost seven o'clock on the East Coast. They're probably up by now. If not, it isn't too early to wake them."

"Shouldn't we check with the hospital first and find

out what's going on with your mother before you call your brother?"

"The hospital isn't going to give out any information over the phone, and if I know Bob Brundage, he'll fly out regardless. The thing is, it may be a challenge for him to find flights out of DC that will get him to Phoenix at a decent hour this evening."

Even though Joanna knew it was urgent to make the call, she sat looking at Bob's name and number in her contacts list for a very long time before actually pressing the call button. Bob was her brother—her full brother with the same two parents—but he was also more or less a stranger. He and Joanna had never met until seven years earlier during Joanna's first year in office. Bob, the result of an unwed teenaged pregnancy, had been born long before their parents married. Given up for adoption and raised in a loving home, Bob hadn't come looking for his birth family until after the deaths of both his adoptive parents.

Joanna had caught sight of him for the first time in the lobby of the Hohokam Hotel in Peoria, Arizona. A good twenty years older than Joanna, Bob had looked so much like their mutual father, D. H. Lathrop, that Joanna had thought at first that she was seeing a ghost. At the time of that first meeting, he had still been active duty military. Since then he had retired from the army as a full-bird colonel, but he and his wife, Marcie, had remained in Virginia, where he had found work with a defense contractor.

Learning that she had a brother had come as a huge

shock to Joanna. It had also been a bitter pill to swallow. Eleanor Lathrop had spent years complaining about the fact that Andrew Roy Brady and Joanna had "gotten knocked up," as Eleanor liked to call it, during Joanna's senior year in high school. For years Joanna had endured Eleanor's criticism for that error in judgment. Since Eleanor knew all too well the cost of giving up a child, her hypocrisy on that score was something Joanna had never been able to forgive.

After Bob and Marcie had surfaced in all their lives, Joanna had maintained a cordial but not particularly close relationship with them. Eleanor, however, thrilled to have her long-lost son back in her life, had been much closer. On a trip back East in their RV, Eleanor and George had spent the better part of two weeks touring DC with Bob and Marcie in tow, or maybe it had been the other way around. Eleanor had come home with albums full of photos from that trip. Joanna had been polite enough to scan through them, but the truth was, every one of the photos featuring the smiling foursome in front of some landmark or other had been a blow to her heart.

"She never looks that happy around me," Joanna had complained to Butch.

"The reverse is also true," her husband had noted. "You don't look that happy around her, either. Give her a break, Joey. Bob was lost to your mom for decades. He lives on the other side of the country, and Eleanor hardly ever gets to see him. Isn't it about time to put this late-breaking case of sibling rivalry to rest?"

With those words of remembered loving advice still

ringing in her head, Joanna pressed call for the number to Bob's cell phone.

"Hello, sis," Bob answered, sounding slightly groggy. "What's up?"

Joanna was taken aback. Even in those few words, his voice sounded so much like their father's that it took her breath away.

"It's Mom," she said without further preamble. "She and George were in a terrible car wreck between Flagstaff and Phoenix late last night. George died at the scene. Mom has been airlifted to St. Gregory's Hospital in Phoenix in guarded condition where she's currently undergoing surgery—for what, I have no idea. Butch and I are on our way there now, driving. I've yet to speak to anyone at the hospital, so I can't give you any more details."

The words had rushed out in a torrent. Now Joanna paused for breath.

"Hang on for a minute," Bob said. "We're still in bed." In the background Joanna heard the sound of several drawers being opened and then slammed shut in rapid succession.

"How come there's never a paper and pencil anywhere within reach when you need it?" Bob muttered. Then after another pause, he came back on line "Okay. What hospital did you say?"

"St. Gregory's in Phoenix. As I said, Butch and I are on our way there, but we're only just now on the far side of the Divide. We won't be at the hospital for a couple more hours at least. As soon as I have a chance to talk to

Mom's doctors, I'll get back to you. But I thought you'd want to know about the situation right away."

"I do," Bob answered. "Definitely. We're not that far from Reagan International. I may be able to get a direct flight out of there sometime later today, but I'm not sure. What happened again?"

"According to what I was told, George was at the wheel when he ran full-speed into one of the bridge piers on a freeway overpass on I–17 just south of Camp Verde. The RV was smashed to pieces and then rolled down an embankment. What I don't understand is why they were on I–17 in the first place. It's the long way around if you're coming from Minnesota."

"Eleanor said something about that when I talked to her a couple of weeks ago," Bob answered. "She said they were going to visit some friends in Salt Lake and then drive back by way of Zion National Park and the North Rim of the Grand Canyon."

Funny, Joanna thought, stifling a sudden burst of anger. *She never mentioned that plan to me, and neither did George.*

"Okay," Bob was saying. "Let me get on the horn and see what I can do about plane tickets. At this point, I don't know if I'll be coming solo or if Marcie will be along. That depends on whether or not she can get off work. I'll call you as soon as I know my ETA."

"Will you want us to pick you up?"

"No," Bob said. "Don't bother. Whether Marcie's with me or not, I'll rent a car. Are you driving or is Butch?"

"Butch is."

"Tell him to take care."

"Don't worry," Joanna said. "He is."

She hung up then. "According to Bob, Mom told him weeks ago that they'd be coming home by way of Zion and the Grand Canyon. How come nobody said a word about that to me?"

Butch reached over and patted the back of Joanna's hand. "Good question," he said, before adding, "Sorry."

Joanna knew he was—sorry, that is. Taking Butch's relationship with his own extremely challenging mother into consideration, there could be no question that he understood Joanna's situation all too well.

"I should probably call Marianne next," Joanna said. The words were barely out of her mouth, and she was in the process of scrolling through her recent calls, when the phone rang. Marianne Maculyea's name and number magically appeared in the caller ID screen.

The Reverend Marianne Maculyea and Sheriff Joanna Brady had been best of friends from junior high on. As pastor of Bisbee's Tombstone Canyon United Methodist Church, Marianne had seen Joanna through some difficult times, and Joanna had done the same for Marianne. It wasn't at all surprising that she would be one of the first to call, especially in view of the fact that Marianne functioned as the local police and fire chaplain.

"Great minds," Joanna said into the phone, smiling in spite of the bleakness of the situation.

"Tica Romero just let me know what's happened," Marianne said. "I'm so sorry. What can I do to help?"

"There's not much to be done at the moment," Joanna said. "Butch and I are driving to Phoenix right now to check on Mom. As far as we know, she's still in surgery. Jenny's looking after Dennis, and I'm sure Carol Sanderson will be glad to help out as needed."

"What about final arrangements for George?" Marianne asked. "I know a thing or two about those. Maybe I can help on that score."

"Before anything can be done about final arrangements, the body will need to be released from the morgue, most likely the one in Prescott, and transported to a local funeral home. No telling how long that will take. The real problem is, I don't have any idea which of George's friends and family will need to be notified. I'm sure my mother had all those details at her disposal, but I'm completely in the dark."

"All right," Marianne said. "But remember, once you need me to work on this, I'm ready, willing, and able."

"Thank you," Joanna said.

There was very little traffic on the road. With their police escort, they sailed through Tombstone, St. David, and Benson, barely slowing down from highway speeds. On the far side of Benson and on I–10 westbound, flashing lights on the shoulder of the road let them know the next tag team of police vehicles was ready to take over.

"Let them know we'll have to stop off at the Triple T for a minute or two," Joanna told Jaime before the Pima County officers took their respective positions. "The baby is crowding my bladder, and I can only go so far before I have to stop."

As they sped on through the night, Joanna slipped her phone back into her bra. "I don't know who else to call," she said.

"Don't call anyone else until we know more," Butch advised. "In the meantime, why don't you recline your seat and close your eyes for a few minutes? This is going to be a tough day. You're going to need as much rest as possible."

He didn't have to tell her twice. Joanna was sound asleep when they pulled into the truck stop parking lot fifteen minutes later. While she went into the restroom, Butch refilled their traveling mugs. They were in and out of the place in less than five minutes.

"What if she doesn't make it?" Joanna asked quietly, when they were once again under way.

"We'll have to hope she does, but in the meantime, we'll need to call off the party. Those are the next people you should call," Butch added. "Jim Bob and Eva Lou."

Jim Bob and Eva Lou Brady were the parents of Joanna's first husband, but when Butch had turned up in Joanna's life, they had welcomed him with open arms and treated him as a spare son-in-law. As for Dennis? Denny Dixon may not have been a blood relative of theirs, but as far as Jim Bob and Eva Lou were concerned, Denny was as much their grandchild as Jenny was. And Joanna never doubted for a second that this new baby would be treated the same way.

"It's still early," Joanna said, trying to put it off.

"No," Butch said kindly. "They'll want to know sooner than later. My guess is Eva Lou will be at the house to cook breakfast before Jenny and Denny have a chance to crawl out of bed."

When the phone rang and Jim Bob answered, Joanna was relieved to spill out the story to him rather than to his wife. Eva Lou knew too much about the complex relationship that existed between Joanna and her mother. It was easier for her to hear reassuring words coming from Jim Bob.

"Don't worry," he said. "We'll go about canceling the party. I believe Eva Lou and your mom have been e-mailing back and forth on the guest list, so getting in touch with all those people won't be a problem. If you want us to stay here and look out for the kids we will, but if you need us to come to Phoenix to backstop you, just say the word."

"Thank you," Joanna murmured.

For a long time after that last call Joanna stayed quiet, looking out through the passenger window as the moonlit desert flowed by outside their speeding vehicle. She and her mother had been at war for as long as Joanna could remember. In the last few years, Joanna had come to understand that much of their conflict had been due to the fact that, once Joanna's father died when she was fifteen, Eleanor was the last parent standing in their family.

D. H. Lathrop had been mostly exempt from doing the hard work of childrearing. While he was alive, he'd worked far too many hours, and once he was dead, her father was completely off the hook. In Joanna's eyes, he had grown to be someone of mythic proportions—perfect in every way—while Eleanor, the one left running the show, had somehow morphed into her daughter's version of evil personified.

In the last few years, helped by Butch's insightful observations on the topic, Joanna had come to recognize that D. H. Lathrop had been anything but perfect and Eleanor wasn't pure evil, either. But there were still substantial obstacles that prevented Joanna from accepting Eleanor as she was, warts and all. These days it was easier for Joanna to see how difficult it must have been for her hidebound mother to deal with raising a headstrong daughter. More than once their screaming arguments had ended with Eleanor saying, "I hope you have a daughter just like you someday."

Which hadn't happened. Through the luck of the parenting draw, Joanna had ended up with Jenny, a smart, kind, helpful kid—an honor roll student with a devotion to horses rather than boys—something for which Joanna was profoundly grateful. Right now, about to head off for college, Jenny was older than Joanna had been when she'd had her daughter.

Riding along in silence, Joanna began formulating what she would say to her mother. First, of course, she'd need to tell her that George was gone. And then she realized it was time for her to apologize—for a lifetime's worth of bickering, misunderstandings, and wrangling.

"A penny for your thoughts," Butch said.

Joanna answered with a little white lie. "I'm thinking about how to break the news about George to Mom."

"Tough duty," Butch said.

"And I'm thinking about how I've always been too

hard on her," Joanna added. "Maybe it's time I tried to dial some of that back."

"Good idea," Butch agreed. "No time like the present."

They were a ways north of the Gila River before Joanna's phone began ringing off the hook as people from inside the department learned what had happened. After having to tell the story over and over again and hearing countless "so sorries," Joanna ended a call from Homicide Detective Ernie Carpenter and then switched off her phone.

"I can't do this anymore," she said to Butch. "Besides, once I know what's going on, I'm going to need to call all these people again anyway to update them on Mom's condition."

"You can call them back, or I will," Butch said. "You're not in this mess alone, babe, and don't you forget it."

The sky was beginning to lighten in the east as they approached Phoenix, having driven there in a little under three hours flat. It was time for the cop part of Joanna Brady's heart to take over for the daughter part. Turning on her phone, she dialed Tica's number.

"Who investigated the accident?" she asked.

"I thought you'd want to know that. Highway Patrol—a guy by the name of Arturo Davis. He was the initial officer on the scene, and a Yavapai County deputy named Blake Yarnell was the second to arrive. George's remains have been transported to the Yavapai County Morgue in Prescott. Would you like me to text you all those numbers?"

"Please," Joanna said. "That would be a big help."

"I'll get right on it."

"And, Tica?"

"Yes?"

"Thank you for sending Jaime Carbajal to give me the news. That was incredibly thoughtful."

"It's what the department does for complete strangers, Sheriff Brady," Tica reminded her. "Why wouldn't we do it for you?"

When they arrived at the entrance to the hospital, the escorting cop cars turned off their lights, blinked their headlights, and melted into the early morning traffic. Butch pulled up into the porte cochere and stopped in front of the sliding glass doors.

"You go on in," he said. "I'll find a parking place and join you in a minute."

Joanna entered the marbled lobby and walked over to the reception desk. "I'm here to see Eleanor Lathrop Winfield," Joanna said. "My name's Joanna Brady; Eleanor is my mother."

The woman behind the counter typed some letters into her keyboard and then frowned at the information that appeared on her screen. "If you wouldn't mind taking a seat here in the lobby, the doctor will be right down."

Suspecting bad news, Joanna nodded and retreated to a small seating area near the front entrance. When Butch showed up a minute or so later, she waved for him to join her.

"What's up?" he asked.

"The doctor's on his way down."

"That's not good," Butch observed.

Just then an elevator door slid open and a tall, rangy man in scrubs entered the lobby, swiveling his head as if searching for someone. When the clerk behind the counter gestured in Joanna's direction, he came straight over as Joanna stood up to greet him.

"My mother?" she asked.

He shook his head. "She didn't make it," he answered quietly. "We lost her in the OR. Her injuries were too extensive. Since we knew you were already on the way, we decided to wait until you arrived to give you the news."

"No," Joanna said. "This can't be true."

She stumbled blindly backward toward her chair and might have fallen had Butch not been there to guide her.

"Because of the circumstances, Ms. Brady, there will have to be an autopsy. The accident occurred in Yavapai County, so we've notified the ME there to have someone come and collect the remains."

"Can I see her?" Joanna asked.

The doctor glanced questioningly in Butch's direction before he replied. "It would be good to have a positive identification," he said, "but I'm not sure that's wise. Your mother was in a high-speed roll-over accident. She has multiple cuts, contusions, and abrasions. The visible damage is quite extensive and shocking."

"I'm a police officer," Joanna said quietly. "I want to see her."

Shrugging, the doctor pulled out his pager. "This is Dr. Collins. Please move the deceased patient, Mrs. Winfield, into a room on the seventh floor," he said. "Her daughter is coming up, and she'll need some privacy."

"Do you want me to come, too?" Butch asked.

"No," Joanna said, passing him her phone. "I'll do this alone."

"Are you sure?"

"Yes, but while I'm gone, try calling Bob. If we can catch him before he gets on a plane, we should. With autopsies and MEs involved, it may be several days before we can make any plans for funeral services. He may want to hold off on his departure for a day or two."

"Okay," Butch said. "I'll call Bob first; then I'll call the kids."

"Thank you," Joanna whispered, not trusting her voice.

As Dr. Collins headed back for the elevator, Joanna hurried to keep pace. "Your mother had no idea that her husband was gone," he said. "We were afraid the shock would be too much for her, so we didn't give her that information. Turns out that telling her would have made no difference. Her internal injuries were simply too extensive."

Joanna should have been full of questions, but she was numbed to silence.

"There is one thing, though," Collins added. "She was unconscious when they brought her into the ER. Once we were up in the OR and the anesthesiologist was about to put your mother under, she came to for a moment. It was difficult to understand her, and it's possible she wasn't entirely lucid, but she was fussing about a red dot. She wanted to be sure we told you about it."

"What red dot?"

"I have no idea. Perhaps we're wrong about what we thought she said, but since she was so focused on it— almost frantic about it—I wanted to be sure to give you the information."

The elevator opened on the seventh floor, and Dr. Collins ushered Joanna into a long tiled corridor. The walls were done in a pastel shade of peach. Framed pieces of original artwork hung on the walls between doorways. The place looked more like an art gallery than a hospital.

Most of the doors were open with patients, visitors, or nurses visible inside the rooms. Dr. Collins stopped in front of one the closed doors. "Your mother's in here," he said. "Take as much time as you need."

Joanna forced herself to step over the threshold and then stood still for a calming moment, steeling herself for what was to come, as the door whispered shut behind her. Her mother's still form lay under a sheet on a rolling hospital bed. Joanna took a single cautious step forward. As she approached the bed, Joanna was horrified. Eleanor's face had been so badly pulverized that she was barely recognizable. Someone had shaved off a chunk of hair in order to stitch up a jagged cut that ran from the middle of her scalp to the top of her eyebrow. A living Eleanor Lathrop, who had prided herself on never stepping out of her house without every hair carefully in place, would have been horrified.

Joanna stood in silence for what seemed a long time. Then, even though her mother was clearly beyond the reach of her voice, she found herself speaking aloud. "George is gone, Mom, and so are you," she said softly.

"And I'm so sorry—sorry that you're gone and sorry for everything I ever did to drive you nuts."

That was what Joanna had come to say and it was all she had to say. She fell silent, as if waiting for Eleanor to respond. After all, Eleanor had always been the one to have the last word. And it seemed as though she did this time, too: the red dot. In an instant of amazing clarity Joanna knew exactly what Eleanor's frantic comments about the red dot meant and why her mother had so desperately wanted to be assured that Joanna would get the message.

Turning on her heel, she reached for her phone, but of course it wasn't there. She had left it down in the lobby with Butch. A nurse stood in the corridor just outside the door, as if waiting to see if Joanna required any assistance. The woman seemed startled when the door slammed open, and Joanna bolted past her.

"Is there anything else you need?" the nurse asked.

"No," Joanna said. "Thank you. I'm done here."

She paced impatiently in front of the elevator, pushing the button over and over, until the door finally opened. She found Butch in the lobby exactly where she'd left him, her phone pressed to his ear.

"Here's Mom now," he said when he saw Joanna sprint off the elevator. "I need to go." He hung up. "What's wrong?"

"I need the phone," she said.

It took her browser only a few seconds to locate the number for the Yavapai County Sheriff's office. She had met Sheriff Gordon Maxwell at law enforcement conferences. He wasn't someone she knew well, and right now she wished she did. The operator who took the call, after ascertaining this was not an emergency, eventually put it through to the sheriff's office. There another gatekeeper tried her best to redirect Joanna's call. "The sheriff is rather busy this morning. Could his chief deputy help you?"

"I don't want the chief deputy," Joanna said firmly. "This is Sheriff Joanna Brady from Cochise County. I wish to speak with Sheriff Maxwell himself."

"Please hold."

"What's going on?" Butch asked.

Before she could reply to Butch's question, Sheriff Maxwell came on the line. "Sheriff Brady," he said. "I was just now reading the overnight reports and learned that your stepfather died in last night's roll-over accident on I–17. I'm so sorry."

"That's why I'm calling," Joanna said quickly. "I don't believe it was an accident, and George Winfield isn't the only victim. My mother, Eleanor, died in the OR shortly before I made it to the hospital."

"You think it's homicide?" Maxwell asked. "I've got the report right here in front of me. Dr. Winfield slammed into the overpass at full speed. No skid marks. No sign of any braking. Officers on the scene said there was no sign of alcohol, but given the victim's age, it might have been a medical emergency. What makes you think otherwise?"

"When is the autopsy?" Joanna asked.

"Gavin Turner, our ME, was out of town over the weekend, so he's a little backed up. He's got two cases in front of Dr. Winfield's at the moment. With all of them presumably natural causes, he'll most likely do them in the order in which they arrived."

"A suspected homicide would move to the head of the queue, wouldn't it?"

"Yes, but ..."

"I think the autopsy is going to reveal that George Winfield was shot to death by someone wielding a rifle complete with a laser targeting system. I've seen how badly mangled my mother's body was. If George's body was in similar shape, it's possible the entry wound was overlooked during the initial investigation. After all, it was the middle of the night, and he was already dead. People see what they expect to see. If the EMTs on the scene regarded George as an old codger who had suffered a heart attack or stroke, it's not likely they would go looking for a bullet wound."

"A laser sight?" Maxwell asked. "Where is all of this coming from?"

"My mother," Joanna said. "She regained consciousness briefly as they were taking her into the OR. She insisted that they tell me about the red dot."

"But she didn't specify which red dot?"

"No, but how many important red dots are there in the world? I think the dot appeared on George's chest. The next thing you know, kerblamo—they slammed into the overpass."

Gordon Maxwell was silent for a moment. "Okay, then," he said. "This changes things. I'll give Doc Turner a call and see if he can move Dr. Winfield's autopsy to the head of the line. And I'll get my homicide guys on the case, too. This means we'll need to take a look at the wreckage in a whole new light. DOT has shut down the overpass while they examine it to make sure it's still structurally sound, but if this is a crime scene, we'll need to take a much closer look in daylight hours."

"Thank you," Joanna said.

"Give me your number," Maxwell said. "Depending on what shows up in the autopsy, my chief homicide detective, Dave Holman, will be in touch." Then, after a pause, he added. "So sorry for your loss."

"Thank you," Joanna said. She had heard those words so many times today that her response was almost mechanical. "But for right now let's concentrate on catching the SOB who did it."

"Yes, ma'am," Maxwell said. "I couldn't agree with you more."

Joanna ended the call and then looked anxiously around the lobby, searching for a restroom.

"Right over there," Butch said, reading her mind and pointing. "I'll be right here when you finish. Then we're going to go have breakfast and talk."

By the time they left the hospital, Joanna's phone had registered fourteen voice mails, including two separate messages from Marliss Shackleford of the *Bisbee Bee*. Joanna didn't bother playing any of them right then. She wasn't ready.

"What did Bob say?"

"That he'll hold off on coming for now, but that both he and Marcie will be here for the funerals."

"That makes sense."

"Jim Bob and Eva Lou were already at the house when I called Jenny, so they got the news at the same time she did. It's a good thing they were on hand. Jenny has been a brick, but she fell all to pieces when I told her. I'm glad Eva Lou was there to take charge."

"So am I," Joanna said.

They had stopped at a Denny's on Indian School and had chosen a booth as close to the back of the restaurant as possible. "I took the liberty of calling Burton Kimball," Butch said, once the waitress had delivered Butch's coffee and taken their order. "I hope you don't mind. I remembered George mentioning that Burton had drawn up their new wills a while back, and I thought he should be in the know."

"Good call," Joanna said. "No telling how long it would have taken for me to get around to that."

"According to Burton, he has letters regarding their wishes for final arrangements, and naturally, Higgins and Sons is the mortuary of choice."

Joanna nodded. "No big rush on that score," she said. "The bodies can't be released for burial until after the autopsies, and Mom's body is still here in Phoenix."

"What should we do then?" Butch asked. "Go back home? Stay here in Phoenix? What?"

"I want to go to Prescott," Joanna said. "When the autopsy report comes through, I want to be on hand to see what it says. And then I want to go to the crime scene up by Camp Verde. I want to see for myself where it happened."

"Aren't you too close to this?" Butch asked. "In addition to which, you're outside your jurisdiction and have zero official standing."

"The fact that I have no official standing in the investigation is the only reason I *can* go there," Joanna countered. "I'm already off work. Right now we're two hours away from Camp Verde. If we go back to Bisbee, we'll be six hours from there. I want to go now and get the lay of the land firsthand. We'll be home tomorrow. That'll be plenty of time to start dealing with final arrangements."

"Tell me about the red dot," Butch said quietly.

Joanna bit her lip. "Dr. Collins told me about it on our way up to the room. He said Mother was frantic to be sure I was told about it. At first none of it made sense to me. And then, when I was there in the room, standing next to the bed, it suddenly became clear. She must have seen a laser dot on George just before it happened."

Unbidden tears started again. "I wanted her to be alive when I got there," Joanna said, choking back a sob. "I wanted to tell her I was sorry for being such a problem child when I was growing up. I don't know what I was hoping for—most likely not a Hallmark moment. Maybe I wanted her to tell me I was forgiven and that maybe, just maybe, she was proud of me and of what I've done with my life."

"She was and she did," Butch said quietly.

"Did what?"

"Told you that she was proud of what you've done with your life. When the chips were down, she entrusted you with a precious gift—that red dot. She must have known you were smart enough to find out what really happened last night. Sometimes, Joey," he added, "actions speak louder than words."

For the first time since she had tumbled out of bed hours earlier, Joanna smiled. "Did anyone ever tell you you're a very smart man?"

"Not recently," Butch said as the waitress brought their food. "And not nearly often enough."

By 11:00 A.M. they were in the lobby of the Yavapai County Medical Examiner's office in Prescott. The equipment in the morgue may have been up to the minute, but the hard-backed wooden chairs in the lobby came from a much earlier era. Told by a receptionist that Dr. Turner was currently unavailable, they had been seated for the better part of ten minutes when a lanky man in a sports jacket hurried into the room, glancing at his watch as he came.

The new arrival was obviously a known entity. "Hey, Dave," the receptionist said. "How's it going?"

"I'm running late. Doc will have my ears."

Dave had to be Dave Holman, Joanna realized. As he moved toward an interior door, she was hot on his heels. "Detective Holman?"

"Who are you?"

"Sheriff Joanna Brady from Cochise County," she said. "George Winfield was my stepfather. Eleanor was my mother."

"Eleanor of the red dot?"

"That would be the one."

"I won't have any information until after the first of the autopsies is completed. In addition to which, since this is part of an ongoing investigation . . ."

"Save your breath, Detective Holman. I know the drill, but I also know a little about extending professional courtesy to fellow officers. And since I voluntarily came forward with important information in this matter . . ."

"Possibly important information," he responded.

Joanna drew herself up to her full five-foot-four, which was a good nine to ten inches shorter than the detective. "Are you a gambling man, Detective Holman?"

"I suppose. Why do you ask?"

"You go right on in there and observe Dr. Turner's autopsy, but if it turns out I'm right and my stepfather was shot to death, then I expect some respect from you and some consideration as well."

"Yes, ma'am," Detective Holman said. "Now, if you'll excuse me . . ."

He disappeared through the door.

When Joanna looked back at her husband, Butch was grinning. "Obviously not a poker player," he commented.

"At least he hasn't played poker with me," Joanna replied, smiling in spite of herself.

Knowing they were stuck in the waiting room for an hour at least, Joanna picked up her phone and began returning calls. By now Marliss Shackleford had left three separate messages, so Joanna started there, wanting to start by getting the worst of the bunch out of the way.

"I'm so glad you finally got back to me."

The word "finally" grated. "As you can well imagine, Marliss," Joanna said carefully, "this has not been my best day for returning phone calls."

"Is it true both George and Eleanor are gone?"

"Yes," Joanna answered, "both of them. George died at the scene of an accident on I–17. My mother passed away in the OR at St. Gregory's Hospital in Phoenix earlier this morning."

"Have the next-of-kin notifications been done so we can go ahead and run the story?"

That stopped Joanna cold. Marliss had always purported to be such a great friend of Eleanor's, but now the truth was out. She didn't even have the decency to express her condolences. Friendship or not, for her this was now all about the story.

"My mother's side of the family may have been notified," Joanna said. "But I don't have any idea about George's. I'd hold off on the story if I were you."

"But we have a deadline . . ."

Joanna cut Marliss off in mid-objection. "Oops, sorry. I have another call." The truth was, she did have another call, one with a number she didn't recognize. Right then, talking to an aluminum siding pitchman was preferable to dealing with Marliss. She switched over to the other line.

"Joanna?"

"Yes. Who is this?"

"Ali—Ali Reynolds. I just heard about your folks. One of our employees, Stu Ramey keeps one ear glued to a police scanner day in and day out. When your name was mentioned in regard to a roll-over that occurred on I–17 last night, Cami, Stu's assistant, recognized it and called me right away. Is there anything at all I can do to help?"

Months earlier, Joanna and Ali, a retired television news anchor now living in Sedona who was also a partner in her husband's cyber security company, High Noon Enterprises, had been thrown together into the investigation of a hijacking operation involving stolen LEGOs. The situation had devolved into a whole series of homicides as the gang of hapless crooks had turned on one another. In the process, Cami had very nearly lost her life when one the hulking thugs had literally yanked her out of a borrowed cop car through an open window.

"I'm surprised my name came up over the radio," Joanna said. "But yes, the two victims are my mother and stepfather. George Winfield died at the scene. My mother passed away at a hospital in Phoenix earlier this morning."

"That's appalling," Ali breathed. "You must be in shock. If you're coming this way for any reason and need a place to stay, please know that you're welcome to come here."

"Thank you," Joanna said, "what a generous offer. Butch and I are in Prescott right now awaiting the results of the first autopsy. I doubt my mother's remains have made it as far as the morgue."

"Dr. Turner is good," Ali told her without prompting. "He's a careful guy who'll do things right."

Joanna knew that Ali had worked for the Yavapai County Sheriff's office at one time, so it wasn't surprising that she would know the ME. Could she maybe also give Joanna the inside scoop on Detective Holman?

"You wouldn't happen to know a homicide detective named Dave Holman, would you?"

Joanna was surprised when Ali laughed aloud. "As a matter of fact, I do. Dave and I were actually an item back in the day, but we both got over it and married other people. How do you know Dave Holman?"

"He just went into the morgue to witness my stepfather's autopsy."

"He's a homicide detective," Ali objected. "Why would he be involved in an MVA?"

"Because it may not have been an accident," Joanna told her. "I believe it's possible that George was shot. With all the carnage on the scene, first responders may not have recognized the entry wound for what it was."

"But what brought you to that conclusion?" Ali wanted to know.

"Because of my mother," Joanna answered. "She came to just as she was being wheeled into the OR and was babbling about a red dot and wanting the surgeon to promise that he'd tell me about it."

"A laser sight?" Ali asked.

"That's what I think."

"What does Dave think?"

"He thinks I'm full of it."

"Well, if Dave is wrong, he'll be the first to admit it. But if this is a homicide, why would George . . . ?"

"Winfield," Joanna supplied.

"Why would he and your mother have been targeted? What does George do?"

"He retired several years ago. Before that, he served as

the ME in Cochise County. My mother was a housewife. And I don't think this is a matter of someone deliberately targeting them. They were snowbirds on a return trip to Arizona from Minnesota. I can't imagine how anyone would have known where or when they'd be passing through Camp Verde. Even I didn't know they were coming home by way of the North Rim until this morning, after it had happened."

"So you're thinking it's random then?"

"Yes," Joanna said. "Like that shooter who held Phoenix freeways hostage last summer."

Over the summer Phoenix freeways had been plagued with a series of random shootings. No one had died in any of those attacks, and a suspect was currently in custody.

"Could be a copycat," Ali suggested.

"That's what I'm thinking, too," Joanna said.

"If you're at the morgue now, where are you going after that?"

"Depending on the autopsy, we'll either go visit the crime scene or head home."

"Remember," Ali said, "if you need a place to stay, all you need to do is call."

"Will do," Joanna answered. "But once we visit the crime scene we'll probably hit the road."

She hung up, marveling at the difference between this relative stranger's concern and generous offer to help compared to Marliss Shackleford's callous treatment of the death of her supposedly "best friend."

Joanna's phone rang again immediately. This time

it was Burton Kimball, Joanna and Butch's attorney as well as Eleanor and George's. "I'm so sorry about all this. Butch just called and let me know about what happened. I told him that Higgins was George and Eleanor's mortuary of choice."

"Yes," Joanna said. "Butch told me."

"Were you aware that George and your mother had new wills drawn up just before they left town last spring?"

"I'm sure they mentioned it, but I didn't really pay much attention."

"Both named the other as sole heir in the event one of them preceded the other in death. With both of them gone, however, and other than a small bequest to one of George's nephews, you're their sole heir. Where are you, by the way?"

The fact that Bob had been left out of the equation seemed odd, but now wasn't the time to question it.

"I'm in Prescott right now, awaiting autopsy results on George. I still need to pass the mortuary information along to the ME. If you happen to have contact information for the nephew, I'll need that, too, so the ME can take care of the next-of-kin notification."

"Fax or e-mail?" Burton asked.

"E-mail," Joanna answered. "I have no idea where to find a fax machine up here."

For more than an hour, Joanna responded to one condolence call after another. She spent fifteen minutes on the phone with Chief Deputy Hadlock, making sure everything at the department was in order. Finally the inner door opened, and Detective Holman stepped into the lobby, stopping directly in front of Joanna. "You called that shot," he said.

"I was right?"

"Dr. Winfield suffered a gunshot wound to the chest. In addition, he had multiple other injuries. Those were so substantial, and there was so much blood loss, that first responders failed to locate the entry wound. Since he was declared dead at the scene, they didn't look any closer before initiating transport."

"An entry wound but no exit wound?" Joanna asked.

The door opened again and a gentleman wearing a lab coat and horn-rimmed glasses entered the room.

"I'm Dr. Turner," he said. "And you are?"

"I'm Sheriff Joanna Brady. I'm also George Winfield's stepdaughter."

"I knew George, by the way," Dr. Turner said. "We'd met at conferences here and there. But what you said about there being no exit wound is exactly correct."

"You found the bullet?"

Turner nodded. "A .223," he said.

"That suggests an AR-15 style weapon?" Joanna asked.

"Indeed it does," Turner said, giving Joanna an appraising look. "The bullet entered just below his collarbone and lodged against his left hip."

"He was shot from above then?"

"Yes, the trajectory angle suggests that the shooter may have been on the overpass itself. By the way," Dr. Turner added. "George spoke of you often, Sheriff Brady, and with a good deal of fondness."

"That fondness was a two-way street," Joanna said. "I'm going to miss him terribly."

"I'm sure you will."

Off to the side, Detective Holman cleared his throat. "I'm heading back to the crime scene to reexamine it in light of this new information."

"Can we come along?" Butch asked.

"Who exactly are you?" Holman asked.

"I'm Butch Dixon, Sheriff Brady's husband."

Holman sighed. "I just got my marching orders from Sheriff Maxwell. He says she's good to go, so I suppose you are, too. Come on. Do you want to ride with me, or do you have your own wheels?"

"We have our own. Lead the way," Butch said.

Joanna could tell from the set of his jaw that Detective Holman wasn't the least bit happy about their tagging along, but he had been given orders to include them, and he was following those orders to the letter.

Joanna was gratified to know that professional courtesy counted for something in Yavapai County after all. But it didn't count for much with the Arizona Department of Transportation. I–17 was closed at the General Crook exits, where traffic was diverted around the overpass and then allowed to reenter the freeway at both the north- and southbound entrances. DOT trucks and equipment were parked both on and under the overpass. Most of the workers, all of them wearing orange safety vests, were clustered around the bridge pier on the west end of the overpass. A twisted length of broken guardrail indicated the speeding RV's path as it careened off the roadway and down the embankment.

"Doesn't look good," Joanna observed as Butch parked the Enclave on the shoulder of eastbound General Crook Trail. "With all this activity, there's not much chance of finding any trace evidence."

Holman came over to the Enclave and signaled for Butch to buzz down the window. "I'll go talk to whoever's in charge and see if we can get permission to go up and take a look."

"Not gonna happen," Butch observed as Holman walked away. "When some overpaid grunt from the DOT gets a chance to tell a badge-carrying cop to take a hike, it's not going to turn out well."

And he was right. Holman returned, shaking his head in resignation. "No unauthorized personnel allowed on the overpass or under it until after the structure has been declared sound and given the official stamp of approval."

"But can we look around down here?" Joanna asked.

Holman shrugged. "I don't see why not."

"There were no skid marks?" Joanna asked, getting out of the vehicle. With Holman at her side, she walked as close as possible to the overpass before a worker waved them away.

"None," Dave answered. "There was no indication that the driver made any effort to brake, leaving responding officers to believe that the accident might have been the result of some kind of medical emergency. The RV hit the bridge pier with enough force that the body peeled open like a tin can and sent pieces of torn sheet metal flying in every direction."

Joanna nodded. "And turned it into shrapnel," she said. "I know all about that. I saw the damage to my mother's face and body. No wonder the EMTs missed the bullet wound."

Together Joanna, Butch, and Dave Holman paced northbound on the freeway as far as the exit—the spot where southbound traffic was being diverted—searching every inch of pavement for signs of braking or skidding.

"There are no travel services at this exit," Butch said as they walked back toward the overpass. "Where does General Crook Trail go?"

"Nowhere fast," Dave told them with a laugh. "General Crook was out here battling Indians in the 1870s, and he built a supply road from Payson to Prescott. These days Forest Road 300 generally follows the same route, but there are a few spots along the way where you can see the original roadway."

"It's all dirt?"

"Yup."

"Does anyone live in either direction?"

"Not permanently," Dave answered. "At least they're not supposed to. It's Forest Service land. There are some genuine campgrounds scattered here and there along the trail, but it's possible there are some squatters out there as well, especially at this time of year when it's hot as hell down in Phoenix."

Back at the overpass, they took advantage of the cop directing traffic to cross the frontage road, first in one direction and then the other, walking along both shoulders and looking for signs that someone may have been loitering there and lying in wait. They found nothing of any interest.

"Who called it in?"

"A trucker named Ken Slonaker who was hauling a load of carpet from a warehouse in Salt Lake to a warehouse in Phoenix. He said that your folks' RV passed him about a mile up the road. Their taillights were still in view when he saw them wobble first and then go flying off the road. He stopped at the scene and immediately dialed 911. I took a look at that initial report. He was asked if he saw any vehicles on the road, and he said there was close to a minute before there was any additional oncoming traffic in either direction."

"Was he asked about the possibility of someone being up on the overpass?" Joanna asked.

"The report didn't say, but I can get his contact number. Let me ask."

Just then one of the highway workers came looking for them. "We've checked out the overpass and deemed it structurally sound," he announced. "We'll be letting traffic back through in a couple of minutes. If you want to look around under the overpass or on it, now would be a good time."

On the way back, Dave's phone rang. He listened for a moment. "Great news," he said. "Thanks for letting me know."

He put his phone away, quickening his pace and forcing Joanna to hurry to keep up.

"What?" she asked.

"That was one of the CSIs up in Prescott. I told them to go out to the impound lot and check the RV wreckage for bullet holes."

"And?"

"They found three. Two were in the particle board partition to the bathroom at the back of the cabin. The third was in the captain's chair that would have been directly behind the driver's seat."

"So there were four shots in all?" Joanna asked, and Holman nodded.

"Not much of a marksman," Butch muttered.

"But good for us," Holman said. "The trucker was right there. We know at least four shots were fired . . ."

" . . . and the shooter wouldn't have had time enough to hang around gathering up his brass," Joanna finished.

"Exactly," Detective Holman said. "So let's go find it."

The highway crew, done with their work but glad to have a few more minutes on the clock, joined in the search, one that was entirely successful. Three .223 shell casings were found up on the bridge deck. One was found below, almost hidden from view in an expansion joint.

By then they'd been hiking around in the noonday sun for the better part of an hour, and the heat was starting to get to Joanna. When one of the highway workers passed out cups of ice water from the orange bucket on the back of his truck, Joanna drank one and poured the other one over her hair.

Dave looked at her and frowned. "Are you okay?" he asked.

"She's pregnant," Butch said, explaining what should have been obvious.

"And she's been out here looking for brass all this time?" Dave replied. "Let's get her inside somewhere so she can cool off."

Knowing she was overheated, Joanna didn't object to their talking about her like she wasn't there or to their bossing her around, either. Within a matter of minutes, they were settled in the relative chill of a McDonald's, where Joanna downed several glasses of lemonade in rapid succession, which in turn required an immediate visit to the restroom. She returned to the booth to find Holman and Butch deep in conversation.

"So we're looking for someone who's not an experienced shooter using a rifle with a laser sight," Butch said. "I think that means we're looking for a kid."

"What makes you say that?"

"Depending on the weapon, just the gun itself could weigh up to eight pounds. Add in the sight. What's that?"

Holman shrugged. "Could be another five or six pounds."

"So let's say the shooter is standing up on the overpass," Butch continued. "He's waiting to do the deed and building up his courage to do, but he's also holding the weapon the whole time. When he finally gets around to using it, the damned thing weighs more than he expects because his arm's tired."

"Which might account for the missed shots," Joanna put in.

"And also meaning that the shooter could well be a

kid without sufficient muscle power to actually control the shots," Holman added.

Before anything more was said, Dave's phone rang, and he picked it up immediately. "Yes, Mr. Slonaker," he said. "Thank you so much for calling me back." There was a pause. "Yes," Dave continued. "That's correct. I'm a homicide detective. It turns out the guy in the RV died from a bullet wound."

Knowing Slonaker was the truck driver, Joanna leaned closer, hoping to hear what was being said. She couldn't make out the exact words, but the sounds of distress coming through the phone were clear enough.

"Yes," Dave went on. "You're right. It's a miracle it was them instead of you, but with all of this in mind, I need to ask you a couple more questions. And if you don't mind, I'd like to put you on speaker so I can make notes of what you're saying."

Joanna held up her phone and mouthed the words, "Do you want me to record this?"

Nodding his assent, Dave turned his phone on speaker while Joanna switched hers to record, but Ken Slonaker was still too focused on his own near-death experience to be of much use.

"I almost died last night," he said. "My wife's been telling me for a year now that it's time for me to hang up my keys and retire. Maybe I will. There are nutcases out here killing people for no other reason than they're driving down the road? That's crazy!"

"I couldn't agree with you more," Dave said. "But if we're going to take this guy down, we'll need your help."

"What kind of help?" Slonaker asked, finally managing to get a grip. "You name it; I'll do it."

"You said there was no traffic on the freeway. What about on the overpass?"

"Now that you mention it, I remember seeing a vehicle up there," Slonaker said after a momentary pause. "I saw it driving away as I pulled up. Well, I saw the lights anyway."

"Headlights? Taillights?"

"No, asshole lights," Slonaker replied. "You know, those guys who jack up their four-by-fours until they're six feet off the ground? They're all assholes. They're also the ones who put spotlights on top of their vehicles. They're only supposed to use them off road, but . . ."

"Wait," Dave said. "You're saying you saw a vehicle with those kinds of lights leaving the scene of the crime and didn't mention it earlier?"

"I had no idea this was 'the scene of a crime.' In fact I had forgotten about it completely until just now when you asked. Besides the vehicle wasn't *at* the scene of a crime," Slonaker countered. "He was above it—up on the overpass. Probably didn't even see what happened."

"Can you describe the vehicle?"

"All I saw was what was visible over the guardrail. Pickup truck. No make or model, but a dark color of some kind. Jacked up like that and with the lights on top, I'm guessing a four-by-four mostly used off road."

"Which direction was it headed?" Dave asked.

"Eastbound."

"So what happened when you arrived?"

"I already told all this to the other officers," Slonaker objected.

"I need to hear it, too, if you don't mind," Dave told him.

"Okay, so I saw the RV's taillights swerve up ahead of me. I thought maybe the guy had dozed off or something. Then the lights sort of bucked up into the air when it hit the overpass and then went off the road. I knew it was bad before I even stopped. In fact I called it in before I got out of my truck. The 911 operator wanted to know how many people were involved. That's when I went down the embankment. It took a while for me to find them. They were all the way at the bottom, still strapped in, but cut to pieces. There was blood everywhere. I checked for pulses. The man was already gone. The woman was still hanging in, but just barely. But this was clearly an accident. At least that's what it looked like to me. Now you're saying it's a homicide?"

Joanna touched Dave's hand enough to get his attention, then she shook her head and held a shushing finger to her lips. Dave frowned but he got the hint.

"We're investigating it as a possible homicide," he said.

"Is there anything else?" Slonaker asked.

"Not at this time," Dave said. "If we need something further, we'll get back to you." He ended the call and then looked questioningly at Joanna. "What was all the head shaking about?"

"Has there been any mention in the press that the case is being investigated as a possible homicide?"

"Not that I know of. Our CSIs know about the bullets,

and the ME knows about the gunshot wound, but until he's able to contact Dr. Winfield's relatives and make the notification . . ."

"Call him. Tell him not to mention the homicide aspect until we give the go-ahead."

"Why?"

"We think the shooter might be a kid, right?"

"Maybe but . . ."

"And if we go on acting like we're not investigating a homicide, he may believe he's getting away with it. With any kind of luck, we can trick him into coming back in search of that missing brass."

"How do you propose to do that?"

"We're going to salt the mine," Joanna said.

"How?"

"If you'll give me one of those four casings, we can put it back on the overpass and hope the shooter comes looking for it."

"Nope," Dave asserted. "No way either one of us is going to tamper with even part of this evidence. These casings are familiar. SWAT uses the same kind of ammo at the range. I'll give you four of those, marked so we can use them for positive identification later, but I don't see how this will help us identify the guy. How do you propose to do that?"

"By setting up some kind of temporary surveillance system on that overpass and on every roadway leading to or from it."

"Is that even feasible? If the guy sees patrol cars parked anywhere in the neighborhood, he'll drive right on by."

"I'm not talking cops and patrol cars. It turns out, you and I have a mutual friend—Ali Reynolds. Maybe she can set up some kind of wireless surveillance system that won't be completely obvious to the bad guy. All we need is a plate number on the vehicle. Once we have that, we'll be way ahead of where we are now."

Dave nodded. "I suppose it's worth a try."

Ali's number was in Joanna's recent calls list, and Joanna dialed the number with her phone on speaker. Ali answered on the second ring.

"Are you in Sedona?" Ali asked. "Do you need a place to stay or do you want to come to dinner?"

"Actually, I'm in Camp Verde with a friend of yours, Dave Holman, and we need your help."

"What kind of help?"

"I'm hoping for assistance in setting up a multi-camera surveillance system in a remote location."

"A permanent system or temporary?"

"Definitely temporary."

"To capture what?"

"A vehicle license plate," Joanna answered.

"Where?"

"At the overpass on I–17 at General Crook Trail. That RV wreck this morning was no accident. My stepfather was shot. We're reasonably sure that the shooter was standing on the overpass at the time since we found several pieces of brass up there."

"And you're thinking he'll come back looking for it?"

"Exactly. Once we ID his vehicle, it'll be much easier

to nail him, but the problem is, the location is out in the middle of nowhere, and I have no idea how to pull it off."

"And I suppose you want this done immediately if not sooner?"

"Yes."

"Let me think for a moment," Ali said. Then after a pause, she said, "What about setting up a phony construction zone? Knowing a construction crew is liable to turn up on the scene should give the bad guy a certain urgency in getting back there to collect the evidence. It so happens I have a whole closetful of wireless video cameras right here at our company headquarters in Cottonwood that can be deployed at a moment's notice. The problem is, they all *look* like video cameras. If we put up construction zone barrels and cones, we may be able to conceal the cameras inside them, and slowing traffic will give the gear a chance to capture better images."

"Even in the dark?"

"Yes, but I suspect that's going to require some careful rigging. We'll need some cones and barrels to carve up jack-o'-lantern style so we can see which ones work best with our video equipment. It might also be a good idea to have one or two of those construction generators parked at the site just to make the whole construction scenario more believable."

"There's a Department of Public Works maintenance yard in Cottonwood," Dave said, speaking aloud for the first time. "I can give them a call and let them know that they should give you whatever you need."

"Okay," Ali said. "Camille Lee is the one who will be coming there to pick things up. By the way, does High Noon have a billing entity on this or are we doing it gratis?"

"Send the bill to the Yavapai County Sheriff's Department," Dave said. "I haven't cleared it with Sheriff Maxwell, yet, but by the time you're ready to do the installation, it will be."

He stood up as Joanna ended the call. "Where are you going?" she asked.

"Back to Prescott," he said. "I want to get these casings turned over to the crime lab so they can look for prints. I'll have a deputy pick up some range casings and bring them to you. Where will you be?"

Joanna looked around the noisy McDonald's. What she needed more than anything right then was some peace and quiet. "Just a sec."

She redialed Ali's number. "Is there a chance Butch and I could hang out at your place for a while this afternoon while you get things pulled together?"

"Sure," Ali said. "No problem. I'll text you the address, and I'll give our majordomo, Leland Brooks, a call so he'll be expecting you."

Hanging up, Joanna caught Holman taking a surreptitious look at his watch. She took that as a telltale sign about what he wasn't saying—that he was also due back at the ME's office in Prescott for the Eleanor Lathrop autopsy.

"What about the kids?" Butch asked. "Shouldn't we leave all of this to the people here and head back home?

And we're just going to stop by a relative stranger's house and hang out for a while even though she won't be there?"

"Ali's not a complete stranger," Joanna reminded him. "We both met her earlier. Besides, Eva Lou and Jim Bob are looking after the kids. They couldn't be in better hands. And I need to do something, Butch. I suggested this surveillance thing, and I want to be here to see it through. Either it'll work tonight, or it won't work at all. Besides, I don't know about you, but I'm in no condition to make a six-hour trip back to Bisbee right now."

"Me either," Butch admitted reluctantly. "Maybe we'll have time enough to grab a nap, but I'm not wild about spending the night. If we both get our second wind, I'd rather head home than stay over."

"Fair enough," Joanna said.

When Butch and Joanna arrived at Ali's house on Manzanita Hills Road, they were greeted by a white-haired gentleman with a British accent who escorted them into a cool library where the coffee table was already set with glasses, ice, and two pitchers—one filled with iced tea and the other with lemonade. Joanna poured a glass of lemonade, which she topped off with a dose of iced tea, giving her weary body a jolt of much-needed caffeine.

"If you'd like to have a lie-down in the guest room . . ." Leland Brooks offered.

Sinking deeper into a very comfortable chair and holding her glass in hand, Joanna shook her head. After the plastic furniture and noisy din of McDonald's, this cool, quiet room with its plushly upholstered furniture was nothing short of heaven.

"No, thanks, Mr. Brooks," she said. "This is perfect. I need to return some calls."

"What I need," Butch said, "is a nap. If you don't mind, I'll accept that lie-down offer. It's been a long day so far, and it's liable to get longer."

Joanna watched in surprise as Leland Brooks ushered Butch out of the room, closing the French doors behind them and leaving Joanna alone with her perpetually buzzing cell phone. Part of the problem was that it was almost out of juice. Fortunately she had stowed an extra charger in her purse.

Her first obligation as well as her first call was to the department, where she spent the better part of an hour on the phone with Tom Hadlock, her chief deputy. He had served admirably as her jail commander and was as loyal as an old blue tick hound, but promoting him to chief deputy had been a step too far. Two years into the job, he still required a good deal of hand-holding. One at a time, she walked him through the routine administrative steps that had to be handled on a daily basis in Joanna's absence. Fortunately there had been no incidents overnight or during the course of the day that were anything out of the ordinary.

"I'm going to have to be off on bereavement leave for at least several days," she warned him as they finished the conversation. "That means you're going to have to continue to hold down the fort, but if you need anything— anything at all—day or night, call me."

"Yes, ma'am," Tom said, sounding relieved. "I'll be sure to do that. In the meantime, I'm getting lots of calls from the media asking for a statement about what happened up there. Now that the ME in Yavapai has released both names, what should I tell them?"

"That as far as you know the incident is still being treated as an MVA and the investigation is ongoing. Let it go at that."

"Got it," Tom said.

Joanna asked to be transferred over to her secretary. Kristin Gregovich came on the line in full business mode and then relaxed when she realized who was calling. "I have a ton of messages for you," she said.

"I'm not surprised," Joanna said. "My phone has been ringing off the hook, too, and those calls are from only the people who have access to my cell number. My e-mailbox is also overflowing. I'm trying to respond to both calls and e-mails, but by the time I reply to one, two more show up."

"Do you want me to reply to some of those for you?"

"No," Joanna answered. "I need to handle those myself."

"I suppose you know that Marliss Shackleford is parked outside the chief deputy's door?"

"Hardly surprising, but he should be able to give her a crumb or two now. That may get her off his back."

There was a small pause before Kristin asked, "How long will you be out?"

"Until the end of the week at least," Joanna replied. "In the meantime, I'm counting on you to bolster the chief deputy if he gets in over his head."

"Will do," Kristin said.

Somewhere in the background a doorbell rang. Moments later the French doors opened, and Leland Brooks entered the room, carrying a small manila envelope.

"Excuse me, madam," he said with a formal half bow. "A deputy just dropped this off for you."

"Thank you," Joanna said, unplugging her phone, accepting the envelope, and rising from the chair. "Could you please show me where to find my husband?"

Brooks led her down a short hallway and indicated a closed door. Quietly she cracked the door open. Inside the room, Butch, fully clothed except for his shoes, lay on his side and snored softly. If they were going to head home later that night, sleeping was what he needed more than anything. That way he could drive, and Joanna could sleep.

"I'll leave him be for right now," Joanna told the butler. "If he wakes up, tell him I'll come back for him as soon as I drop these off."

Once behind the wheel, she used the Enclave's Bluetooth capability to dial up Ali Reynolds. "I have the brass, and I'm on my way to Camp Verde," she said. "What's the situation on the cameras?"

"Our people—Stu Ramey and his assistant, Cami Lee—should be at the overpass and putting things in place by the time you arrive. Cami cut small holes in the cones and then taped the cameras inside so their lenses can focus through the peepholes. It'll take some time to set them up, get them properly focused, and bring them on line, but everything should be in place within the next hour or so. I'll be there long enough to check out the installation, after that Dave wants us all to get lost while we wait to see if our guy takes the bait."

"So Detective Holman is coming, too?"

"He just called." Ali said. "He's on his way from Prescott even as we speak."

Approaching the exit to General Crook Trail, Joanna was gratified to see that Ali's people had outdone themselves in setting the "construction zone" stage. A full panoply of orange and black warning signs had been deployed along the shoulder of the freeway—REDUCE SPEED AHEAD; CONSTRUCTION AHEAD; SLOW; FINES DOUBLE IN CONSTRUCTION AREA. Once Joanna reached the exit itself, it was lined on both sides with a collection of cones, as were both sides of the overpass. She doubted all of them contained cameras, but there were enough on display it seemed likely at least one of them would be able to capture the license plate on any passing vehicle. Two construction-style generators were parked on the side at either end of the overpass.

Just off the westbound portion of General Crook, a bright red Prius was parked on the shoulder with a man hunched over a laptop in the front passenger seat. Joanna pulled in behind the Prius as a young woman she recognized as Ali's associate, Cami Lee, returned to the car.

"How's it going?" Joanna asked.

"The angle for each camera had to be manually adjusted, but we're almost there now. Did you bring the brass?"

"Yes."

"Great. Once you put those where you want them, we'll

be sure that some of our cone cameras are aimed at those, too. We're hoping for a license, yes, but also for an image that will be good enough for our facial recognition software."

There was plenty of traffic on the freeway below but virtually none on the overpass itself. After borrowing a pair of latex gloves from Cami, Joanna went about distributing the four .223 casings. If they had been given some kind of identifying mark, those weren't visible. As Joanna found places to conceal them—an expansion joint, a niche beside one of the guardrail uprights, the crack between the pavement and the base of the guardrail—she was struck by a reminder of her mother—out in the yard at High Lonesome Ranch, hiding colored eggs early on a sunny Easter morning. It was a blink of memory only, but enough to make her eyes mist over with tears as she realized yet again that her mother was dead. Eleanor may have been annoying as hell, but it hurt to realize that she was gone. Forever.

Straightening her shoulders, Joanna placed the last of the four casings on the far side of the overpass while Cami followed behind her, readjusting the positions of some of the cones to aim the cameras more effectively.

"About done here?" Ali asked, walking up behind her.

"Just about. That's the last of them," Joanna said. "As soon as Cami finishes with focus adjustments we can go."

They were starting back toward where the cars were parked when a single vehicle exited the freeway and approached the overpass. Joanna and Ali spotted it at the same instant—a jacked-up black Toyota Tundra with a pair of spotlights mounted on top.

"Looks like he's here," Ali shouted. "Show time."

The solo driver at the wheel of the Tundra paused momentarily at the stop sign with his left turn signal blinking. As if suddenly spotting the three people still on the overpass, he gunned the motor. The truck shot straight across General Crook and onto southbound I-17.

"Let's go," Ali shouted, sprinting toward her Cayenne. "Cami, call it in, and then you keep watching from here to make sure he doesn't pull a U-turn and come back northbound."

Ali and Joanna clambered into the Cayenne at the same moment.

"Are you armed?" Ali asked as she fastened her belt and put the Porsche in gear.

"A Glock is all," Joanna said.

"Me too," Ali said grimly. "Up against an AR-15 those won't be worth much, but I don't want to lose him."

After a gravel-spraying U-turn, Ali sent the Cayenne racing down the freeway entrance. It seemed to Joanna that the vehicle shot from zero to eighty-plus in the blink of an eye.

"We called it right," Joanna breathed, scanning the northbound roadway to see if the suspect had maybe doubled back and dialing 911 at the same time. "We called it right. He did come back."

"And it almost worked, too," Ali added. "The problem is, he got there a moment too soon, and now he knows we're on to him."

"Nine-one-one, what are you reporting?"

"A suspect in last night's double homicide is southbound on I-17. He entered the freeway at General Crook Trail."

"May I ask your name and number? And where are you right now?"

"My name is Joanna Brady. I'm the sheriff of Cochise County. I'm currently in a Cayenne pursing the suspect who is most likely armed and dangerous."

"Can you give me your mileage marker?"

As soon as one appeared, Joanna did so.

"I've just notified the Highway Patrol, but I must advise you to leave off your pursuit. You're putting yourself in harm's way."

"This guy is someone who blasts people in their cars from freeway overpasses," Joanna said tersely. "That means there are innocent people out on the road today who are in far more danger than we are."

"Call Dave," Ali said.

Ending the 911 call, Joanna did as she'd been asked and was gratified that Dave didn't bother telling them to mind their own business.

"You're sure he hasn't doubled back?" Dave asked on speakerphone.

"Not so far, but we're watching."

"If he makes it as far as the Sunset Point rest area which is usually full of tourists . . ." Ali said in the background.

"All hell breaks loose and no telling how many innocent civilians could be in danger," Dave replied. "I'm on it. I've got people working on putting up a southbound roadblock before the Sunset Point exit."

"We'll need one northbound, too," Joanna added. "Somewhere on the far side of Camp Verde, just in case."

Joanna glanced at the speedometer. It was hovering around ninety-five as the car darted past lumbering trucks and slowpoke RVs and minivans. All Joanna could do was hope the high-powered Porsche and Ali's driving skills were both up to the task.

Ali's phone rang. She nudged it across the seat for Joanna to answer and then returned both hands to the wheel.

"Ali's phone," Joanna said.

"It worked," a voice Joanna recognized as Cami's reported. "We caught the plate and Stu ran the number. The vehicle is registered to Norma Braeburn of Cave Creek, Arizona."

"They caught the plate," Joanna reported to Ali. "And the vehicle belongs to a woman?"

"Yes," Cami replied, "but there was a male at the wheel. It's likely the vehicle is being driven by Norma's seventeen-year-old son, Scott."

"Has that information been forwarded to the Department of Public Safety and Dave Holman?" Joanna asked.

"Done and done," said Cami.

By then the Cayenne was on a relatively flat plateau approaching Sunset Point. Just then, Joanna caught sight of the Tundra, flying northbound in the opposite lanes.

"The suspect is now headed northbound," Joanna shouted into the phone at Cami. "Call Camp Verde PD and see if they can establish a roadblock on I–17 somewhere north of General Crook Trail. In the meantime, Cami, you and Stuart need to get out of there."

In other places along that stretch of I–17, hundreds of feet of elevation separated the northbound from the southbound lanes. This was one of the few spots where crossing the median was even feasible.

"Hold on," Ali ordered. "We're turning." She moved over onto the left-hand shoulder and hit the brake so hard that the engaging seat belt slammed into Joanna's shoulder and belly. Moments later they bounced across the median on a dirt track and then shot back into the northbound lanes.

"Call Dave back," Ali ordered, unnecessarily, since Joanna was already doing exactly that.

"We spotted him," Joanna reported. "He's north-bound again."

"I know," Dave replied. "Highway Patrol had a car parked just north of the Sunset Point exit to keep him from going in there. The guy took off as soon as he saw the patrol car. He's headed northbound now."

"So are we," Joanna said. "We should be able to see him any minute."

Joanna glanced at the speedometer. With the needle now hovering at well over one hundred, that seemed more than likely.

"There he is!" Ali shouted. "We've got him."

It was true. The Tundra had been boxed in behind a slow-moving semi passing another even slower semi on a steep grade. When the one vehicle finally moved out of the way, the Tundra shot around it, but the pickup had lost its momentum and it couldn't quite regain its former speed.

"We're closing on him," Joanna reported to Dave.

"You two need to stand down now," he replied. "We already know the guy is armed to the teeth. Camp Verde is in the process of assembling a SWAT team to block I-17 in both directions at the first Camp Verde exit. I should be there any minute. I'm on 169 only a mile or so from the freeway."

"Oh, my God!" Ali exclaimed. "He's losing it."

And it was true. With her heart in her throat, Joanna watched as the Tundra raced around a northbound RV and then slewed wildly first in one direction and then the other. As the out-of-control pickup skidded back and forth across both lanes of the roadway, the driver in the RV did his best to avoid an almost inevitable collision. After three more wild wobbles, the Tundra veered to the right. It shot off the road and onto the shoulder, tumbling down an embankment in a manner that was almost a carbon copy of what had happened to George and Eleanor earlier that morning.

"He's off road," Ali reported. "Just south of the Bloody Basin exit."

She pulled over on the shoulder just behind the stopped RV. A shaken and horrified older couple popped out of the RV, pointing to the spot where the overturned Tundra had landed on its roof with its wheels still spinning.

Joanna darted out of the Cayenne. She had seen enough wrecks in her time to doubt this one was survivable.

"Call for EMTs," she ordered Ali, handing her back the phone. "I'm going down the hill to see if I can help."

"What if he's still armed?" Ali asked.

"So am I," Joanna answered grimly. "So am I."

She scrambled down the embankment to the spot where the Tundra had come to rest, upside down, against a sturdy barbed-wire fence. Drawing her weapon as she went, Joanna heard the kid long before she saw him.

"Oh, my God!" he moaned. "It hurts. It hurts so bad. Help me! Someone, please help me out of here."

Knowing that even gravely injured he could still pose a deadly threat, Joanna approached the wreckage cautiously. Then, much to her relief, she spotted the AR–15 on the ground nearby. It had been thrown clear when the tumbling vehicle came to rest. Having the rifle out of play was a huge relief, and it went a long way toward evening the playing field. Still, she worried that the rifle might not be the only weapon involved.

"Oh, God. It hurts. It hurts so bad, and I'm bleeding. Help me."

With the Glock still in hand, Joanna approached the cab from the rear driver's side. "Sir," she said. "Do you have a weapon?"

"Who's there?" he asked. "Can you help me? I need help."

"Do you have a weapon?"

"No. I'm hurt—hurt real bad."

Joanna edged forward far enough to peer around the door frame. The overturned truck's sole occupant, trapped by his seat belt, hung upside down inside the vehicle, bleeding profusely. Realizing he was too badly hurt to pose any threat, Joanna immediately holstered her weapon. Then she reached inside and attempted to release the seat belt. It didn't work. The weight of his body on the belt somehow kept the release from responding. Her hand came away bloodied.

It was a shock to realize that the sticky red stuff came from the man who had killed her mother. But Joanna Brady had sworn to serve and protect, even if the person she was protecting didn't deserve it.

"You've got to get me out of here," he pleaded. "It hurts so much. I can't breathe. Please help me."

"Steady now," she said. "We're here to help."

The sound of falling pebbles behind her told Joanna that someone else had come scuttling down the embankment. "Can I help?" Ali asked.

"I need a sharp knife," Joanna told her.

"Right back," Ali said, disappearing the way she had come.

Unable to free the kid, Joanna turned her attention to his wound. Most of the blood seemed to be coming from a deep gash in his lower calf. Shrugging out of her T-shirt, she peeled off her bra and used it as a makeshift tourniquet around his leg.

"Am I going to die?" the kid sobbed hysterically. "I think I am going to die. I want my mom. Where's my mom? I need her."

How could a cold-blooded killer sound so much like a little lost boy?

"You need to be quiet, Scott," Joanna said. "Save your strength. You've lost a lot of blood."

His eyes focused on her face. "Do I know you? How do you know my name? Is my mom coming? Have you called her?"

Ali came skidding back down the embankment and tapped Joanna on the back. "The RV guy had a seat belt scissors in his tool box," she said handing the implement over to Joanna. "I didn't know there was any such thing. And the ambulance is on its way, coming from Black Canyon City. I don't know how long it will take."

With the powerful little scissors in hand, Joanna eyed the problem. "When I cut him loose, he's going to drop like a rock and may end up getting hurt worse than he already is. Can you crawl in through the other side and help break his fall? Then we'll try to lift him out onto the ground."

"Will do."

Joanna put her face in front of the boy's. His eyes were closed. She was afraid they were losing him.

"Scott," she pleaded. "Stay with me. Can you hear me?"

His eyes blinked open. They were out of focus. He looked around in momentary confusion. "Where am I?"

Joanna worried that if he'd suffered some kind of spinal damage, the very act of freeing him might make things worse.

"Listen to me," Joanna ordered. "We're about to cut you loose now. Can you move your feet?" He did. "Your arms?" He did that, too.

"Am I going to hell?" he asked as Joanna went to work on the seat belt. "I'm so sorry."

"Sorry for what?" Joanna asked.

"I didn't mean to do it. I didn't mean to hurt anybody."

Joanna stopped cutting long enough to switch her

phone to record. Her fingers were sticky with blood, and operating her phone wasn't easy.

"Who did you hurt, Scott?"

"Those people," he said. "Those two old people. I didn't mean to hurt them. I didn't mean for anyone to die."

Biting her lip, Joanna concentrated on the scissors. "What happened, then, Scott?" she asked.

"I just wanted to shoot one of my dad's guns. Mom was spending the night in town. I figured she'd never know. But now she will, won't she? Where is she? Is she coming? Has anyone called her? Please. Can you get her here? I want her. I need her."

"Is this your cell phone?" Ali asked. She had crawled into the truck through the broken window and was holding up what appeared to be an unbroken cell phone.

Scott looked at her and nodded. "Call my mom, please. Her number's in there."

"We'll call," Ali assured him, "as soon as we get you out of here."

The seat belt gave way. As Scott dropped, Ali and Joanna together managed to catch him. Even so, he howled in agony.

"It hurts! Oh, God, it hurts! It hurts! Mommy, where are you? Please, I want my mommy."

He was struggling now, and it was a challenge for the two women to wrestle him out of the vehicle. Joanna was surprised when the guy from the RV stepped up to help. He had come down the embankment carrying an armload of blankets and pillows. Together the three of them eased the boy onto a makeshift bed.

Dave Holman rushed down the embankment in such a hurry that he almost did a face plant. "What do you need?" he asked.

Ali handed him Scott's phone. "Call his mother," she said. "Her number's in here."

Joanna was totally focused on the boy. His face was much paler now. She couldn't tell if that was due to the fact that he was no longer upside down or if he was hurt badly enough that he was drifting away. She leaned in close to him.

"Stay with me, Scott," Joanna urged quietly. "Tell me about your father's guns."

"He died," Scott said, "like a couple of years ago. And he left me all his guns. It said so right there in his will, but Mom wouldn't let me touch them. She says I'm not responsible enough for guns."

She's certainly right about that, Joanna thought.

"It's hard to breathe," Scott whispered. "It's like my chest is too heavy. Like there are rocks on it or something."

For the first time, a bright dribble of blood appeared in the corner of his mouth, confirming Joanna's worst fears. The wound on the leg was bad, but it seemed there might be even worse internal injuries.

"Am I dying?" he whispered, reaching out to take her hand. "Are you an angel?"

Four words. "Are you an angel?"

Here Joanna was, kneeling in the hot desert sun, caring for the young man she knew had killed both her mother and George. And yet she knew, too, that he was just a kid—a scared, clueless kid—who was most likely dying. A kid who without malice aforethought—and mostly with no thought at all—had pulled the trigger, simply to try out one of the guns his late father had left to him.

"No," she said. "I'm not an angel."

"Will God ever forgive me for what I did?"

"Yes," Joanna said quietly, squeezing his hand. "I believe He will. He forgives you, and so do I."

And so do George and my mother, she thought.

His hand went limp in hers. She knew within seconds that Scott Braeburn was gone, but she also knew that the last words he had heard on this earth were the ones he had needed to hear—that he was forgiven. And it turned out they were the ones Joanna had needed to say—to say and believe.

She had responded to a random act of violence with a random act of kindness. She had returned good for evil. Somehow that was as it should be. After all, that was how she had been raised. And she knew in that moment, too, that her parents—all three of them—would be proud of her.

Sometime later, an EMT tapped her gently on the shoulder. "Excuse me, ma'am," he said, "we need to check him out."

"It's too late," she replied, reaching out to close Scott Braeburn's staring eyes and then brushing tears from her own. "It's over now. He's gone."

"And before you go up top," he added, "you might want to put your shirt back on."

Looking down Joanna was astonished to see that she was completely topless. While the EMT averted his gaze, Joanna grabbed her shirt and dragged it on over her head. Then she got to her feet and staggered toward the embankment. Another EMT stopped her as she passed. "You might want to use one of these," he said, nodding toward her bloodied hands and offering her a Handi Wipe.

"Thank you," she said. Several Handi Wipes later her hands were mostly clean, and she made her way back up to the roadway. Ali and Dave Holman stood on the passenger side of the RV. Dave stepped away from the group as she approached. "Are you all right?" he asked.

Flushing with embarrassment at having been seen half dressed by Dave Holman as well as the EMTs, Joanna took the cell phone from her pants pocket and turned off the recording app.

"Scott Braeburn is gone," she said. "He also confessed. He said he was just trying the gun out and didn't intend to kill anyone."

"Do you believe that?"

Joanna thought for a moment before she answered. "I do. He was just a kid, a stupid kid with no idea about the real consequences of his actions. I recorded the confession, by the way. It's all here on my phone. Will you need the phone itself or will I be able to take it home?"

"The suspect is dead?"

Joanna nodded. "Yes."

"Then just send me the audio file," Dave said with a shrug. "Since we won't be needing to use it in court, the file will be fine."

By then Ali had joined them in time to hear the tail end of the conversation. "Are you all right?" she asked now, echoing Dave's previous question.

"I'm okay," Joanna said. "But I'm glad the press wasn't here a few minutes ago."

"Right," Ali said with a grin. "Photos like that would make for a very interesting reelection campaign. Now how about a lift back to your car?"

"Yes, please."

"Good work, Sheriff Brady," Dave said as he opened the passenger door to help her enter. "You did what you could for him. No one can ask for more."

"Thank you," she said, giving him a hug.

Joanna and Ali said little on the trip back to General Crook Trail. Nothing more needed to be said.

"I'm assuming you won't be spending the night," Ali said when Joanna exited the Cayenne.

"Thanks, but no," Joanna said. "Butch and I should head home. The kids need us."

"I'm not surprised," Ali said with a smile. "I thought that's what you'd say. But you might want to stick around the house long enough to take a shower and change clothes. Right now you look like you've been in a knife fight."

"Fortunately I packed an overnight bag," Joanna said.

"How will all of this go over with Butch?" Ali asked.

"He's used to me by now," Joanna said. "Nothing I do really fazes him anymore."

"Then you're one lucky woman, Sheriff Brady," Ali Reynolds said. "In more ways than one. And so am I."

Back at the house on Manzanita Hills Road, Joanna found Butch sitting in a wicker chair on the shaded front porch.

"Ali called a few minutes ago and told me you got him," Butch said, as Joanna sat down beside him. "But you shouldn't have let me sleep. I would have been glad to go along and help out."

"I wanted you rested in case we ended up driving back home tonight."

"Are we?"

"I hope so."

Butch gave her an appraising look. "What happened to your bra?" he said.

"Used it as a tourniquet," Joanna explained.

"On the guy who killed your mother?"

Joanna nodded. "But he died anyway."

"Doesn't matter," Butch told her. "You tried to save him. That's what counts. Now go inside, take a shower, and change clothes—bloodstain red isn't exactly your color. How soon do you want to leave?"

"As soon as I get cleaned up."

"Okeydokey."

Joanna leaned over and kissed the top of Butch's bald head on her way past. "Did anyone ever tell you that you're a brick?" she asked.

"Thank you," Butch said with a grin. "Coming from you, I consider that as high praise."

Next from J. A. Jance

Cochise County Sheriff Joanna Brady has never
been busier, but her life is about to get even more
complicated when a puzzling new case hits her
department. The bodies of two women have
been found at the base of a nearby peak, known
to Bisbee locals as Geronimo. One victim was
a local teacher and minister's wife, while the
other was a microbiologist—two vastly different
women with seemingly no connections to link
them. As Joanna and her team hunt down
answers, they begin to uncover a web of sordid
secrets and lies—clues that take the sheriff down
a road that leads shockingly close to home . . .
and to a desperate and determined killer.

Keep reading for a sneak preview of

DOWNFALL

Coming soon from William Morrow
An Imprint of HarperCollins Publishers

Prologue

SHERIFF JOANNA BRADY pulled into the parking place in front of the Higgins Funeral Chapel, put her Buick Enclave in park, and then sat staring at the storefront before her, only vaguely aware of her surroundings. Lowering clouds blanketed the Mule Mountains in southeastern Arizona. It was the last day of August. The summer monsoons had arrived early and stayed on, leaving the desert grassland valleys of Cochise County lush and green.

A flash of lightning off toward the east roused Joanna from her reverie with a warning that the skies might open up at any moment. Still she lingered, unready to go inside and face down this awful but necessary task. She was relieved when her phone rang with her husband's name in the caller-ID window. Answering a call gave her an excuse to stall a little longer.

"Hey," she said. "Where are you? I thought you'd be here by now."

"So did it, and we would have been," Butch said, "if not for the huge backup caused by a semi rollover on the I-10 bridge over the Gila. We're in Tombstone right now. If I come straight there, I could arrive before they close, but—"

"No," Joanna said firmly. "Take Denny home. A funeral home is no place for a five-year-old. I'll handle this on my own."

"You're sure?"

"I'm sure," she said, reaching for the door handle. "I'll see you at home."

She switched her phone to silent and stepped out of the SUV just as the first fat raindrops splattered down on the hot pavement. As soon as the moisture dampened nearby overheated creosote bushes, the air came alive with the unmistakable perfume of desert rain. Most of the time, Joanna would have rejoiced at that distinctive aroma, but not today. Instead, she crossed the sidewalk and opened an all-too-familiar door.

She had come to the Higgins Funeral Chapel for the first time as a teenager, arriving there with her mother, Eleanor, in the aftermath of her father's death. D. H. Lathrop had been changing a tire for a stranded family when he had been struck and killed by a passing vehicle. Then Joanna had come here alone nine years ago. On that occasion she had been a widow, making funeral arrangements for her newly deceased husband, Andrew Roy Brady. And this time?

A week earlier, in the dead of August, life had been as normal as Joanna's life could be, considering she was a busy county sheriff with a daughter heading off to college, a five-year-old son starting kindergarten, and a baby girl due to arrive in early December. That normal had been shattered by a three A.M. phone call that had rousted her out of bed with the news that her mother, Eleanor Lathrop Winfield, and her stepfather, George Winfield, had been involved in a serious vehicular accident while driving their RV home to Bisbee from a summertime sojourn in Minnesota.

George died at the scene; Eleanor had perished after being airlifted to a Phoenix-area hospital for treatment. In the ensuing investigation, Joanna discovered that what had originally been regarded as a simple traffic accident was anything but. A troubled kid, wielding a high-powered rifle with a laser scope, had stationed himself on a highway overpass south of Camp Verde, where he had fired at passing vehicles. With the help of a relatively new friend, Ali Reynolds, Joanna had helped search for and eventually find the shooter.

While attempting to elude his pursuers, the boy had crashed his 4x4. Less than twenty-four hours after George and Eleanor's murders, Joanna had found herself kneeling on the ground at the injured boy's side, comforting their dying killer. Now she was left cleaning up the rest of the bits and pieces. The remains had finally been released by the Yavapai County Medical Examiner's Office. The mortuary had called earlier that day to say that the bodies had arrived in Bisbee shortly after noon.

A discreet chime sounded in a distant room as Joanna opened the funeral home's Main Street door. Norm Higgins, dressed in his customary suit and tie, appeared silently in the doorway of an office just to the right of the entryway.

"I've been expecting you, Sheriff Brady," he said, giving her a stiff half bow. "So sorry for your loss. How can we be of service?"

He ushered her into an old-fashioned wood-paneled office where a single file lay on the polished surface of an ornate antique desk. "I took the liberty of glancing through your mother's file," he said. "At the time of your father's death, your mother purchased two adjoining plots at Evergreen Cemetery. According to this, she was opposed to cremation and wished to be buried in the plot next to your father's. As far as your stepfather's wishes are concerned, however, we're completely in the dark."

"That makes two of us," Joanna said, withdrawing a piece of paper from her purse. "In going through George's things, I located this letter saying that he wished to be cremated and have his ashes scattered near his cabin at Big Stone Lake in Minnesota. The problem is, this letter predates his marriage to my mother. Just today I've learned that my mother has been negotiating with the Rojas family, the people who own the plots next to my parents' plots, in hopes of purchasing the nearest one for George's use. Presumably he had changed his mind about cremation."

She didn't mention how she had learned about the cemetery-plot situation because, the truth was, it hurt like hell. Joanna certainly hadn't heard about it from Eleanor herself. No, that bit of vital intelligence had been gleaned in a phone call with her brother, Bob Brundage—a brother, born to her parents out of wedlock and given up for adoption long before Joanna was born. After the deaths of both his adoptive parents, Bob had come looking for his birth family. Once reunited, he and Eleanor had gotten along like gangbusters. And the fact that her brother had been privy to her mother's final wishes when Joanna herself had not was something that still rankled. In fact, Joanna had heard about cemetery situation for the first time, earlier this morning, mentioned in passing when Bob had called to let her know when he and his wife, Marcie, would be flying in from DC on Tuesday.

What am I? Joanna had wanted to ask while they were still on the phone. *Chopped liver?* Why had her mother chosen to tell Bob all about what was going on when it was Joanna, the daughter with boots on the ground, who would most likely be expected to oversee the arrangements? Why was she the one who had been left in the dark? Joanna's feelings had been hurt, but she hadn't said anything to Bob about it. After all, it wasn't his fault.

"Did it work?" Norm Higgins asked, bringing Joanna back to the present conversation and perhaps repeating a question he had asked previously.

"Did what work?"

"The negotiations to buy the plot."

"More or less," Joanna said. "I mean, my brother was able to reach an agreement on the deal this morning. He expects to have the certificate of purchase in hand by tomorrow afternoon, but I'm not at all sure that's how I want to handle this, and that's what I need to discuss with you. My mother specifically said she wanted to be buried rather than cremated? You're sure about that?"

"Yes," Norm replied, patting the file but not bothering to open it and verify the information. "Her position in that regard is quite clear."

"What am I supposed to do, then?"

Norm Higgins drummed his fingers on top of his desk. "We have a situation where we have reason to believe that Dr. Winfield and your mother wanted to be buried together even though there was no separate plot currently available. On the other hand, we have a handwritten document indicating his wish to be cremated."

"So what do you suggest?" Joanna asked, rephrasing her earlier question.

Norm shook his head. "Quite frankly, Sheriff Brady, these kinds of issues are usually resolved by what we commonly refer to as 'the last person standing'. They're the ones who have the final say, as it were."

"In other words, it's up to me."

"Exactly."

Joanna took a deep breath. "All right, then," she said. "Here's what we're going to do. Go ahead and cremate George's remains. Put his ashes in an urn, reserving a small portion that Butch and I can scatter at Big Stone Lake later on. I want you to have both the urn and the casket on display during the funeral. At the end of that, we'll put the urn in the casket with my mother. That way Mom and George can be buried together. If my father objects, the three of them will need to sort that out among themselves when they get to the other side."

Norm withdrew a piece of paper from his desk, a form of some kind, and began filling in the blanks. "I trust you're not expecting to have an open-casket service or a viewing, are you?"

Joanna was adamant. "Absolutely not. I saw the damage," she said. "My mother wouldn't be caught dead looking like that."

The unthinking words were out of her mouth before she realized how absurdly true they were. Eleanor Lathrop had always put her best foot forward. Remembering that and the appalling way her mother had looked in the hospital, Joanna forced herself to bite back a sob. If Norm noticed her discomfort, he didn't acknowledge it. No doubt he was accustomed to dealing with people who blurted out inappropriate comments because their emotions had been strained beyond the breaking point.

"Yes," he said, nodding. "That's my assessment, too. There's only so much we're able to do. But placing an urn in the casket is a creative way of handling a complex issue. I believe you mentioned the word 'funeral' rather than 'funerals.' Does that mean you're anticipating a joint service?"

Joanna's cell phone buzzed in the pocket of her blazer. She had turned the ringer to silent when she came inside. Over the course of the last several days, she had been overwhelmed with condolence calls. She appreciated all of them, of course, but the sheer number made it hard for her to think straight. Right now she needed to deal with Norm.

"Yes," she said. "A joint service."

"Here in our chapel or at your mother's church? I believe Eleanor attended the Presbyterian church."

"Here," Joanna said, "and with my friend Marianne Maculyea officiating. How soon could you schedule it?"

Norm leaned back in his chair. "We keep a very limited number of caskets and urns in stock," he said. "If you were to make your selection from those, we would have more flexibility. Otherwise, scheduling would depend on how soon we could receive the shipments."

"Assuming I find something suitable in your inventory and choose from those?"

"In that case, I would suggest scheduling the funeral for late Friday morning—say eleven or so," Norm suggested. "Doing it as early as Thursday would make it difficult to get notices to the local media. We handle all of those, by the way," he added. "The notices, I mean. That's part of our comprehensive service. And I'll need to get bio information from you on both your mother and Dr. Winfield in order to write the obituaries. Or would you rather do that yourself?"

"I'll provide the info," Joanna said, "but I'd rather someone else did the writing. And when you post those notices, please mention that the service itself will be private, by invitation only. I'll give you a list of the people who should be there. What I don't want is to have a bunch of outside gawkers show up just for the fun of it."

Joanna's phone buzzed again. Whoever had called earlier had just left a message. She ignored the message notice just as she had ignored the call.

"How much will all this cost?" she asked. "And how soon do I need to pay?"

"Let's worry about that after you've selected the casket and urn," Norm said, rising to his feet. "We expect payment in advance, of course. Once you've made casket and urn selections, I'll be able to prepare an invoice, and since we'll be holding only a single service, I'm sure you'll find the charges reasonable. This way, please."

Back in the mortuary's warehouse section, Joanna found precious little to choose from—at three distinct price points. Knowing her mother would have been pissed if any expense had been spared, and since Bob had agreed to split the funeral expenses fifty-fifty, Joanna opted for the high-priced version—for both Eleanor and George, putting the whole bill on her Visa. Finished at last, she staggered out of the mortuary an hour and a half after entering. It was dark now—well past closing time. Norm unlocked the front door to let her out and then locked it from the inside and closed the security shutters behind her.

Relieved that the funeral-planning ordeal was finally over, Joanna stood on the sidewalk and took a deep breath. The air was cool and fresh. The rainstorm had come and gone, leaving the streets wet and shiny under the glow of recently illuminated streetlights. Runoff from the rain was still draining away, flowing down Brewery Gulch, across Main Street, and into the storm gutter—known locally as the Subway—where Joanna had once done hand-to-hand battle with a killer.

Her phone buzzed with a text from Butch:

Come home. Making dinner. You need to eat to keep up your strength.

After sending a text back saying she was on her way, she scrolled through her recent calls. The last one had come from her chief deputy, Tom Hadlock.

She listened to his voice mail. "Sorry to bother you at a time like this, but we've got either a double homicide or a murder/suicide. Can't tell which. Can you give me a call?"

Joanna ground her teeth in frustration. Tom had served admirably as her jail commander, but she worried that promoting him to chief deputy had been a mistake on her part. He was still out of his depth in certain situations, and this was clearly one of them. She dialed him back immediately.

"What's up?"

"A couple of kids out climbing Geronimo east of Warren late this afternoon found two bodies at the base of one of a cliff—two females. No visible gunshot or stab wounds. Looks like they either jumped or were pushed. One of them seems to have had a campsite set up at near a water hole at the base of the peak, and we found ID in a purse at the campsite. The name on the ID is for one Desirée Wilburton. Apparently she's a grad student from the University of Arizona. The other victim had no identification of any kind. I know you're on bereavement leave, but—"

"Never mind that," Joanna said. "I'm coming. Who all is at the scene?"

"Right now, just the original responding deputy. The two boys who found the bodies are still there as well. Dr. Baldwin is on her way, coming from the far side of Benson. Dispatch is in the process of notifying the on-call detectives, the Double C's."

Kendra Baldwin was Cochise County's relatively new medical examiner. The term "Double C's" was departmental shorthand for Detectives Ernie Carpenter and Jaime Carbajal, Joanna's longtime homicide investigators.

"All right," Joanna said, looking down at her clothing. "At the moment I'm not dressed for hiking either to or around a remote crime scene. I'll need to go home to change and maybe grab a bite to eat. You should probably call in a couple of extra deputies as well. Who all is on duty?"

"Jeremy Stock is close by. He's in the process of finishing up a traffic stop on Highway 92 near the San Pedro. Armando Ruiz is somewhere between Elfrida and Willcox. I'll call both of them and let everybody know that you're coming. The ME is still more than an hour out, so there's no big hurry. You know the way?"

"The front side of Geronimo or the backside?" she asked.

"Front side," Tom answered.

For generations of Bisbee kids, climbing that distinctive double-humped limestone peak east of town had been a rite of passage. Locals referred to it either as Geronimo or else by the name Anglo pioneers had given it—Black Knob. In official topo-map parlance, however, it was referred to as Gold Hill. Too short to be officially labeled a mountain, the limestone peak with a top that resembled the top of a valentine, clocked in at 5,900 feet, 400 higher than the desert surrounding its base. Viewed from the streets of Old Bisbee, Gold Hill stood in the distance like a lonely gray sentinel, towering in the background over the flat expanse of a rust-colored mine-waste tailings dump.

Joanna was personally acquainted with Geronimo, having climbed it twice—once with a long-ago Girl Scout troop and once with her first husband, Andy Brady shortly before the two of them married. Both times she had scrambled up the rocky front of the mountain on her hands and knees and slid back down, most of the way on her butt. Both times she'd been in trouble with her mother afterward for wrecking her clothes.

The front side of Gold Hill was accessed through an old cattle ranch whose entrance was, unsurprisingly, at the end of a street called Black Knob. The backside was approached via a primitive dirt track that ran past a now mostly deserted rifle range. Both routes required four-wheel drive most of the way and a hike for the last half mile or so.

"Okay," she said. "Where are you right now?"

"Still at the Justice Center."

"Give me half an hour to go home and change, then come out to the ranch with my Yukon and we'll drive to the crime scene in that. No way am I going to take my Enclave there. It doesn't have a scratch on it at the moment, and I fully intend keep it that way."

Chapter 1

"Do you have to go?" Denny whined, pushing his macaroni and cheese around on his plate. "Why do you always have to work?"

"Your mommy has an important job," Butch explained. "People are counting on her to do it."

Changed into a regulation khaki uniform augmented by a pair of sturdy hiking boots, Joanna shot her husband a grateful glance. She'd called him on her way home, and he'd had her dinner on the table when she arrived.

Butch, more than anyone, understood Joanna's unstinting commitment to her job. She hadn't run for office with the intention of being sheriff in name only. From the moment she was elected, she had made it a point to be at the scene of every homicide that had occurred inside the boundaries of her far-flung jurisdiction. Just because she had spent most of the day grieving the deaths of her mother and stepfather and planning the funeral service didn't mean she was going to abandon her official duties, especially when a possible double homicide had turned up less than ten miles away from her home on High Lonesome Road.

On the other hand . . . the disappointment registered on Denny's face represented every working mother's all-too-familiar tug-of-war.

"Finish your dinner, Denny, and get your jammies on," Joanna suggested. "Maybe I'll have time enough to read some Dr. Seuss to you before Chief Deputy Hadlock comes by to pick me up."

With a gleeful shout, Dennis hopped down from his chair, cleared his dishes, and then scampered off toward the bedroom with their two dogs—a rescued Australian shepherd named Lady and a stone-deaf black Lab named Lucky—hot on his heels.

"He's tired," Butch remarked, "and so am I. It was a long haul back and forth to Flagstaff, but I think we did the right thing. It's a lot more important to have Jenny settled in her dorm and Maggie in her new stable in a timely fashion rather than expecting Jenny to hang around here for the funeral and end up being late for her first college-level classes. Starting her freshman year that way might leave her feeling like she's behind everyone else from the very beginning."

Joanna nodded. The truth was, it hadn't required all that much effort to talk Jenny into taking a pass on her grandparents' funeral. Not that she didn't care about them—she did. In fact, she had doted on George, and in many ways, she had enjoyed a better relationship with Eleanor than Joanna ever had. By the end of August, most of Jenny's friends had gone off at school, and she was ready to follow suit.

"But will she feel guilty later about missing the funeral?" Butch asked. "That's what worries me."

Joanna smiled at him. "She's a freshman in college. She'll be far too busy to feel guilty for very long."

Dennis returned with his book, his "blankie," and two very devoted dogs. "You go read," Butch said. "I'll clear up."

Joanna and Dennis snuggled into an easy chair in the living room. *Green Eggs and Ham* was Dennis's all-time favorite book, and it wasn't so much a case of Joanna reading the book aloud as it was a responsive reading, with Joanna beginning each sentence and Dennis finishing it. At this point he wasn't actually reading the printed words. He simply knew the whole book by heart.

Two pages from the end, Chief Deputy Hadlock turned up. He stayed in the kitchen with Butch long enough for Joanna and Dennis to finish the story. Then, even though it was still a little before seven, Dennis was ready to brush his teeth and go to bed.

"You do that," Joanna told him, kissing him good night. "Daddy will come tuck you in." Out in the kitchen, Tom Hadlock, hat in hand, stood just inside the back door as if uncertain of his welcome.

"Any news?" Joanna asked.

"The storm we had this afternoon played havoc with the roads. Right now Gold Gulch is running bank to bank, so going by way of the rifle range is out of the question, and from what I hear, the other route isn't much better."

"We should get going, then," Joanna said, giving Butch a quick hug. "See you later."

"Stay safe," he said.

She nodded. It was what he always said when she headed out for duty, and she knew he meant it every single time.

Dusk fell as they drove back toward the highway on High Lonesome Road. There had been enough rain this summer that usually dry washes had been running trickles of water most of the time. Forty-five minutes earlier, after the drenching but fast-moving storm, swiftly flowing muddy water had been hurtling through several recently installed culverts. Now the high water had mostly subsided—at least right here. That was one of the things that made flash floods so dangerous. They were unpredictable. They could arrive with no warning and with no rain in sight, flowing downhill from a storm miles away. The good thing about them was that they disappeared almost as quickly as they came.

"Sorry about calling you out on this," Tom apologized.

"Don't give it another thought," Joanna assured him. "After all, a potential double homicide counts as serious business, and we'll need all hands on deck on this, mine included."

As they drove toward the crime scene, Tom brought her up to speed. Earlier in the afternoon, two boys, thirteen-year-old Marcus Padilla and his younger brother, Raul, had left their home in Bisbee's Warren neighborhood and set out on a hike, planning on doing a little skinny-dipping in the water hole that summer rains had left behind in a natural basin near the base of Geronimo.

According to Tom, Marcus and Raul had evidently pulled the same stunt several times over the course of the summer, and they were accustomed to having the area all to themselves. This time, however, they discovered a red Jeep Cherokee parked at the end of the roadway. Closer to Geronimo itself and near the water hole, they had come upon a seemingly deserted campsite that included a tent, bedroll, and camp stove along with a selection of cooking and eating utensils. Worried about running into the camper, the boys had given up on the idea of skinny-dipping. They decided to climb the mountain instead, hoping to get up and down before the threatening rainstorm arrived. As they started their ascent, they discovered the two bodies, lying one on top of the other at the base of a rocky ledge. With no service available on his phone, Marcus climbed high enough on the mountain to locate a cell signal. Once he had one, he called 911.

"That was when?" Joanna asked.

"About four," Tom said.

"But if the ME just now got there ..."

"My fault," Tom said. "When Larry Kendrick called me from Dispatch and told me he had a couple of kids on the line, I thought at first it was a prank. It's the end of summer when bored kids can get up to all kinds of mischief. So I asked for someone from Patrol to drop by and check it out. By then it was raining pitchforks and hammer handles. Took some time for Deputy Marks to get there. The Jeep was unlocked and the kids had taken shelter inside it to get out of the rain."

"With a thunderstorm like that brewing, those kids shouldn't have been up on the mountain in the first place," Joanna said.

Tom nodded. "There is that," he agreed, turning off Highway 80 and onto the Warren Cutoff. Once in town, they turned a wide left, drove up and over Yuma Trail, and then turned left again onto the dirt-track ranch road. As soon as they did so, they could see the bright glow of generator-powered work lights used to illuminate crime scenes.

Tom's cell phone rang. With effort, he wrestled the device out of his hip pocket and glanced at caller ID. "Oh no," he groaned. "Not her again."

"Marliss Shackleford?" Joanna guessed.

Marliss was a reporter for the local newspaper, the *Bisbee Bee,* which, against all odds, was still going strong both in print and online. At the paper, Marliss functioned as both as star reporter and columnist. In her column, *Bisbee Buzzings,* Marliss often took issue with local public officials, and Joanna's department was a common target for her derogatory coverage, even though she and Joanna's mother had been close friends for years.

"Yup," Tom replied. "The very one."

"Don't answer, then," Joanna advised. "Until we have a better idea of what we're up against, we're better off ignoring her."

"What if she shows up at the crime scene?"

"Considering current road conditions, that doesn't seem likely," Joanna said. "If she does show up, we'll deal with her then."

A mile and a half later, the dirt track ended abruptly in a clutch of parked official vehicles. The last one in line was the ME's Dodge Caravan. "The Jeep on the far side of the wash evidently belongs to one of the victims," Tom explained, putting Joanna's Yukon in park. "She must have hiked in from there, and we'll have to do the same."

"How come?"

"The wash," Tom answered. "A little while ago I was told it was running four feet deep."

Taking Tom's Maglite with her, Joanna hopped out and walked forward to see for herself. Shining the beam into the wash, she saw that the water had subsided. If it had been running four feet deep earlier, now it was down to only a foot or so. It could most likely be forded on foot, but that entailed climbing up and down perpendicular embankments on either side of the running water. Once a vehicle splashed down one of those steep edges, driving up the other side would be impossible. No wonder all the vehicles were parked on this side rather than closer to the crime scene itself.

Joanna returned to the Yukon and to the luggage compartment, where she retrieved her own Maglite as well as a pocketful of latex gloves. When she stepped off into the swiftly flowing water, she gratefully accepted Tom's offered hand, which kept her from being swept off her feet. Once on the far side, both she and Tom had to sit down and empty sand and water out of their boots before continuing on to the crime scene.

By now, the clouds had rolled away. Pinpricks of stars gleaming in the dark sky did little to illuminate the rock-strewn pathway. Neither did the tiny sliver of waning moon. As they approached the grove of trees surrounding the water hole, Joanna caught a glimpse of crime-scene tape.

"We need to go around," Tom explained. "That's where the campsite is."

Beyond the water hole, the ascent began in earnest. It was gradual at first, but as the path became steeper, Joanna found herself panting. Not only was she eating for two these days, she was evidently breathing for two as well.

Partway up the mountain, they had to halt and step off the path in order to make way for several people who, armed with their own flashlights, were making their way down from the crime scene. The momentary pause gave Joanna a much-needed chance to catch her breath. Once the newcomers drew near, she recognized Deputy Jeremy Stock accompanied by two dark-haired boys.

"Meet Marcus and Raul Padilla," Deputy Stock said. "They're the witnesses who found the bodies."

"I'm Sheriff Brady," Joanna said, moving the Maglite from one hand to the other in order to greet the boys properly. "Which of you is Marcus?"

"I am," the taller one said.

"And I'm Ruly," the second one chirped. "I'm the one who saw them first. It was gross."

"I'm told their mother is beside herself with worry," Deputy Stock explained. "The detectives are still busy at the crime scene. The ME just got here, and Ernie is too busy to talk to the boys right now. He asked me to take them home. Ernie and Detective Carbajal will stop by their house later to do an official interview when their parents can be present."

"It's just our mother," Ruly volunteered. "Our parents are divorced. Dad doesn't live with us anymore."

The older boy jabbed the younger one with his elbow as if to silence him. "They don't have to know that," he said.

"You go on home with Deputy Stock," Joanna urged. "I'm sure your mom is worried sick, but thank you for calling 911, Marcus. Some people would have just walked away from something like this without reporting it for fear of getting involved."

"It's okay," Marcus mumbled.

"All right," Deputy Stock said. "Let's get moving."

While the three of them continued down, Joanna glanced up toward a place where the artificial glow cast by work lights illuminated the crime scene, leaving the enormous shadow of Geronimo looming in the background. Another quarter mile of hard climbing brought Joanna and her chief deputy to the base of a massive limestone cliff that soared skyward. Just outside the circle of light, they ran into Deputy Armando Ruiz, who was dutifully stringing crime-scene tape from boulder to boulder.

Stepping into the light, Joanna joined a busy group of people, hard at work on their appointed tasks. Dr. Kendra Baldwin, the ME, was on her knees next to a what looked like a heap of bloodied clothing but that, on closer examination, proved to be something barely recognizable as two intertwined human forms. Detective Carpenter hovered in the background, keeping an eye on everything, while Dave Hollicker—the male member of Joanna's two-person CSI unit—snapped an unending series of crime-scene photos.

"Evening, Joanna," Kendra said, rising to her feet and coming forward to greet the newcomers while stripping off a pair of latex gloves. She was a tall, spare African American woman with a ready smile and a down-to-earth way about her. "So sorry to hear about your mom and George," she added. "Are you sure you're up for this?"

Joanna nodded. "Thank you," she said. "I appreciate your concern, but I'm here to do the job. What have we got?"

"Two females," Kendra replied, looking back at the bloody tangle of victims. "One, Desirée Wilburton, is age twenty-seven. The other probably is mid thirties or maybe a little younger. Rigor suggests they've been dead for twenty hours or so, but I'll be able to give you a more definitive time frame once I have them back at the lab. The stage of decomp suggests that both victims died at about the same time. Desirée wore a watch, which is still running, by the way. She wasn't wearing a wedding ring, but the other one was. Probably the easiest way to sort out who she is would be to check missing-persons reports."

Joanna nodded. "You mentioned a name—Desirée Wilburton. You already have a positive ID on her, then?"

"Tentative," Kendra corrected. "ID was found in a purse inside the tent back at the campsite. In addition to her driver's license, she was carrying ID that identifies her as a teaching assistant for the University of Arizona. Detective Carbajal is in the process of contacting the campus cops there to see what, if anything, they can tell us. So far we have no information at all on the other victim."

"Cause of death?"

"Initially, I'd have to say multiple blunt-force trauma to the head for both of them."

"From being hit with something?"

Kendra shook her head. "No, the injuries I'm seeing so far are all consistent with a fall. No visible gunshot or stab wounds that would indicate the use of a weapon."

Joanna nodded, thinking about how, once George had been extricated from the tangled wreckage of the RV, the immediate assumption had been that his injuries had been caused by the wreck itself. Only Eleanor's insistence on the presence of a "red dot" had convinced Joanna that George Winfield had been shot by someone using a laser sight, and a subsequent autopsy had proven that to be true. Perhaps something similar would occur here, and further investigation of the remains would reveal the use of a weapon of some kind.

Joanna stood in silence, studying the distorted heap of tangled limbs and clothing. Years earlier, encountering sights and smells like this would have sent her racing for the nearest restroom, retching her guts out. Tonight, though, she stood her ground. Carrion eaters and insects had been hard at work devouring the remains for what seemed to be the better part of forty-eight hours. Remnants of clothing revealed that one of the victims—the one on top—was apparently dressed in sturdy hiking boots, jeans, and a long-sleeved khaki shirt. The one on the bottom wore a pair of shorts, a tank top, and a single lightweight tennis shoe. One was dressed to be outdoors roughing it; the other was not.

Jaime Carbajal entered the circle of light, descending from somewhere on the hillside and pocketing his cell phone as he came.

"Had to gain some elevation before I could get a signal," he explained. "According to the U of A, Wilburton is a Ph.D. candidate in microbiology. She's originally from Louisiana. She came to Arizona first as an undergrad and stayed on to earn a master's and is close to finishing up her doctorate. The guy I spoke to says he'll get back to me later with whatever next-of-kin information they have on file, but probably not before tomorrow morning."

"Thanks, Jaime," Joanna said before turning her attention to Ernie. "Any theories, Detective Carpenter?" she asked.

"I'm coming down on the side of murder/suicide," he replied. "From the looks of things, I'd say Desirée had been camping here for a while—a day or two at least and possibly more. The other victim, her girlfriend maybe, drops by. They get into some kind of argument—a lovers' quarrel perhaps. One thing leads to another, and they both end up dead."

"Is there any way to figure out exactly where they were when they fell?"

Jaime shook his head. "Before that rainstorm there might have been physical evidence—maybe even footprints—that would help us determine that. As it stands, we've got nothing." He glanced back at the cliff face rising straight up behind him and then at the ground below. "The thing is, when you're dealing with such hard-packed, rocky terrain, you don't have to fall very far to end up with this kind of catastrophic outcome."

"What about the boys?" Joanna asked. "Is it possible they were involved in some way?"

Ernie shook his head. "I don't think so," he said. "The kids look like innocent bystanders to me," he said. "Because they took shelter in the Jeep during the storm, we went ahead and took their prints for elimination purposes. Just to be sure, Casey ran them through AFIS. Not surprisingly, nothing turned up on either of them."

Casey Ledford was the other member of Joanna's CSI team—her resident fingerprint expert. With newly upgraded computer capability installed on all the patrol cars, it didn't surprise Joanna to hear that the fingerprints of both boys had already been run through the national Automated Fingerprint Identification System.

"What about the vics'?" Joanna asked.

"Considering the decomp, those may or may not be retrievable. In any case, Dr. Baldwin prefers to take prints once she has the bodies back at the morgue."

"Her job, her rules," Joanna conceded.

"Hey, how about somebody giving us a hand here?" Ralph Whetson asked, coming into view while lugging a metal-framed stretcher designed to transport bodies.

Ralph was Dr. Baldwin's morgue assistant and a constant complainer. He dropped his load just inside the circle of light, as if carrying it another step was more than he could manage. Seconds later, someone else appeared behind him. The newcomer was Deputy Stock, also loaded down with a stretcher.

"Hey, Jeremy," Ernie called out, his tone stern and thunderous. "I thought I told you to take those boys back home to their mother."

"You did," the deputy agreed. "I was on my way to do that very thing when I ran into Ralph here and Detective Howell. I could see that Ralph needed a hand. He was trying to carry both stretchers by himself and wasn't making much progress. Deb offered to take charge of the boys so I could help Ralph with the stretchers."

Deb Howell was Joanna's third homicide detective. She hadn't been on call that night, but Joanna knew she was a self-starter. It was hardly surprising that she would turn up at the scene on her own.

Ernie Carpenter, on the other hand, tended to be a bit of a grouch on occasion. From his point of view, orders weren't something that could be casually handed off to someone else. Given that he was close to the top of the department's pecking order, his grumbly bear persona meant that he wasn't always on the best of terms with Joanna's patrol deputies. Knowing this, she stepped in to smooth things over.

"Good thinking," she said. "Carrying those stretchers may be challenging now when they're empty, but it'll be a whole lot more difficult once they're loaded. Seems to me we're going to need all the help we can get."

Ernie favored her with a grudging nod. "Okay," he said.

Dr. Baldwin moved away from the bodies. "Glad you're here, Ralph," she said. "I think we're ready to rock and roll. Let's load 'em up and head 'em out."

About the Author

J. A. JANCE is the *New York Times* bestselling author of the J. P. Beaumont series, the Joanna Brady series, the Ali Reynolds series, and five interrelated thrillers about the Walker Family, as well as a volume of poetry. Born in South Dakota and brought up in Bisbee, Arizona, Jance lives with her husband in Seattle, Washington, and Tucson, Arizona.

Discover great authors, exclusive offers, and more at hc.com.